Red Snake

I pressed my face into the moist, soft moss as I heard them approach, holding my breath until it felt like my lungs would explode. At last their footsteps receded along the trail and I lifted my head and listened as they went on. I had first heard them coming as their feet had struck the granite outcrop a good distance away. At first I thought my mind was playing tricks on me when they came in sight a half-mile away. They had white skin and were wearing clothes of a kind and color I had never before seen or imagined. On their feet were hard shoes, not moccasins. They carried long sticks in their hands and wore hats on their heads.

The Indians with them were not strangers to me, but were not of my immediate tribe. They were to become known as the Wyandot. Many times they had traded with my people and were friends. They were known to us as "the people by the big river." I soon realized that I could be seen and hid myself in a clump of sweet fern near the trail. Even with the smell of the sweet fern, I could smell a very bad odor coming from the white people, whose smell was not at all like the Indians. There were five white people and thirty Indians. They were sweating and grunting with the labor of walking the steep part of the trail and spoke in angry tones, since the black flies were at their worst at this time.

This was the beginning of the fifth moon of our year (May). The Indians carried many bundles and canoes, so I knew they had come by water and were portaging to the big lake. It suddenly came to me that they were probably going to my village, and panic struck me for my people.

Red Snake

George McMullen

Foreword by
Ann Emerson

For information, write:

Hampton Roads Publishing Co., Inc.
891 Norfolk Square
Norfolk, VA 23502

Or call: 804-459-2453
    FAX: 804-455-8907

If this book is unavailable from your local bookseller, it may be ob-
tained directly from the publisher. Call toll-free 1-800-766-8009 (orders
only).

ISBN 1-878901-58-3

10 9 8 7 6 5 4 3 2 1

Cover design by Patrick Smith

Printed using acid-free paper in the United States of America

TO THE MEMORY OF J. NORMAN EMERSON
or
Norm my friend
and to
my wife Lottie, who has been an
inspiration to me.

MR. GARAD.

HOPE YOU ENJOY THIS STORY -

Contents

FOREWORD

This is an unusual book, because it was told to a living person by someone who does not at present inhabit a physical body. In my experience certain people do have the ability to communicate telepathically with entities that once lived on earth but are no longer able to communicate with most of us.

Thousands of such communications have been taken down and printed. There has been an explosion of books and journals that deal with this phenomenon. However, in my reading it has been rare for a humble person living in a little-known time and place to tell his life story just for the sake of letting us of today (and particularly those interested in prehistoric and historic native cultures) know what life there was like and to show us their humanness and fallibilities without any high-blown religious concepts, messages or lessons being included.

George McMullen, the one who will be credited with being the author of this book, has been psychic all of his life and able to see events and communicate with beings in other levels of reality that most of us are quite unaware of. Since this ability was not understood and caused him trouble, he learned to keep this information to himself until, in mid-life, his wife Lottie joined an Edgar Cayce study group and began delving into reincarnation, life after death and other matters in search of a more meaningful kind of spiritual philosophy than her upbringing had provided. George was able to tune into other lives she and he had had and told her so. She then pushed him to use this ability to help others and reluctantly he did so. I was one of Lottie's friends who learned of this ability and sought George out to do an analysis of my husband's physical condition, which was being troublesome.

My husband was Dr. Norman Emerson, an anthropologist. He had been a "stones and bones" archaeologist at the University of Toronto for thirty years, gleaning what could be found out about ancient native peoples from their material remains—fragments of their stone and bone implements, skeletons of animals and birds they had eaten or otherwise utilized, stains in the soil where they had dug pits, had their houses or other structures, remains of their fires. He used to joke that he was a glorified garbage collector because he gleaned so much about their ways of life from their refuse dumps.

I introduced him to George and after they became acquainted mentioned this strange ability. Dr. Emerson decided to test it, and without any information whatsoever gave George an artifact to "read"—the stem from a pipe found on a site abandoned more than 300 years ago. George held the object, concentrated and gradually began telling us of the maker, the way it was made, the meaning it had for its user. He located the place it had come from quite accurately in time and space and even drew a picture of the missing bowl. Uncannily, it was one of the most common types found on that site at that time period, and unlike any George had ever seen. In some strange way he had traced that clay pipe stem back to its source in time and space and learned a great deal about it, much of which could be verified.

Intrigued and impressed, Dr. Emerson took George to a field where we knew there had been an Indian village, though nothing remained to indicate this. George shifted levels and actually seemed to go back in time to when the site was occupied. He could "see" and describe the Indians, smell their campfires, know what they were doing and talking about. To prove it he walked around a house that he could see, although those present could not. They walked behind and put surveyors' pins in the ground where George said the walls of the house were. Then began the painstaking, slow work of scraping inch by inch down through the layers of soil to uncover the secrets it held. It took six weeks of meticulous work to properly excavate the space George had paced around. But there where he said the house was were the brown stains in the soil where the posts had been and it turned out to be the kind of house George had told us he had seen.

This led to many more experiences as Dr. Emerson tried to understand and put to use this unusual talent. Eventually he took George to the site of Cahiague, the historically known capital of the Huron Nation at the time that Champlain visited it in 1615. George was told nothing about what was known concerning the place they were visiting. While there he reported that he was amazed to see so many Indians. He described, quite accurately, the coming of three white men—French—giving details that are not written in Champlain's journals and some that are. I suspect that it was on this trip that George made the acquaintance of Red Snake, the narrator of this story brought through to us by George's ability to contact another dimension of reality that most of us cannot tap.

Dr. Emerson and George McMullen worked together in their space time over a period of several years with fascinating results. Eventually we made a trip to Egypt, Iran and later Israel to check out and validate information that had been given by others with this rare kind of sensitivity. The work came to an end when Dr. Emerson died as the result of a stroke, but George has since worked with other researchers and done some remarkable things.

As I assisted my husband with his research with George and other persons with similar talents, I saw what to me is indisputable proof that certain humans can transcend the limitations of time, space and normal sensory information to "know" past events—some that history has not even recorded—but for which proof is sometimes forthcoming. I personally believe that this book is an actual account of experiences of a Huron who saw the coming of Champlain. You, the reader, will have to judge for yourself. It is a fascinating human story however it comes to us.

ANN EMERSON

INTRODUCTION

This is not my story. It was told to me by Red Snake, an Indian of the Huron tribe, who lived at the time when the French explorer Champlain visited their country. Red Snake was born just before the white men arrived on our shores. He tells the story of one man who lived among several thousand people that were there at that time. He wanted me to write of what he saw and heard, and of his own impressions of how things came about. He is quick to say his is not the only story or impression.

Man was no different then than now; we all have our own ideas, impressions and beliefs that fit our times. Red Snake tells only his own story and not the stories of others. He was an individual, independent and aloof even among his own people. He does not claim to know everything about his village and knows his memory does not recall every detail as it happens, for no one person knows everything that went on. Imagine a town of five thousand people. Think of the politics, competition, love, hatred, jealousy, greed, envy, the haves and have-nots. Sounds like any town in our country today. Towns are made up of people, and that is what the Indians were—just people.

George McMullen

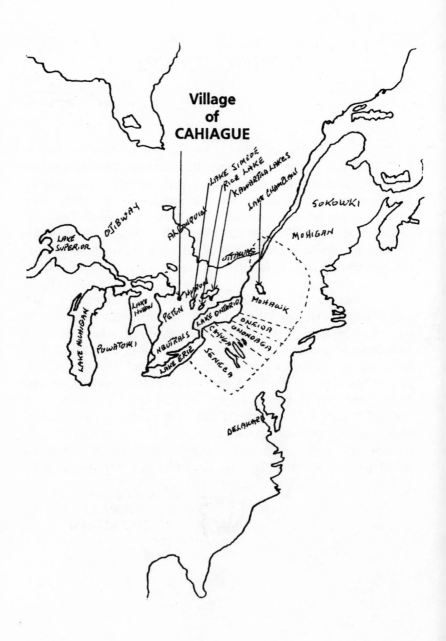

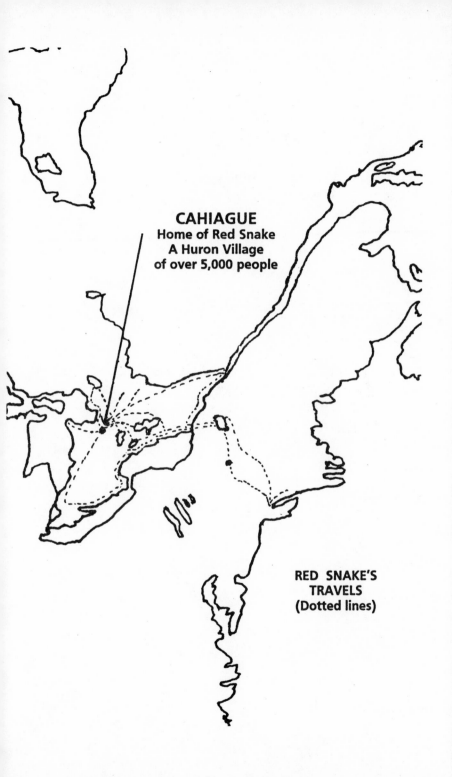

CAHIAGUE
Home of Red Snake
A Huron Village
of over 5,000 people

**RED SNAKE'S
TRAVELS**
(Dotted lines)

1. My Family, My Village

I was born in a large village by the great waters. It was on a small bay opening onto a river which flowed into the great lake. It was very well protected from the open water. There were about five thousand people in the village, and as many as eight thousand when everyone was home on ceremonial occasions. We were part of a larger group of people now called the Iroquois. This was not our true name, as we were from many different tribes and areas. We were called the Huron by the French, but we had many different names within our group. Our village was about forty acres in your measurements, and it sloped slightly toward the water. The west side bordered on the bay; on the north side there was a high, tree-topped ridge. On the west, or top of the hill, were large trees and a palisade. On the south there were trees and an ever-flowing stream and valley palisaded to the bay.

On the lowest level, by the bay, were our longhouses. They were from about fifty to one hundred and twenty feet long and up to thirty feet wide. They were usually about fifteen to twenty feet high and made with poles set close together into the ground. They were covered with bark and the holes were filled with a mixture of mud and moss. Their roofs were made of branches, reeds and grass, or moss mixed with mud. They were under constant repair. Inside the floor was earth, packed down, with fire pits along the middle. There were holes in the roof for light and to get rid of the smoke from the fire pits. This did not always work. I think this is why we were call Red men. We were smoked like meat.

Along the walls were platforms about six or seven feet long by about three feet wide, sometimes larger or smaller. They were used to sleep on or for storing foods or other belongings. They were made of small poles and covered with cedar branches and moss. Skins were laid over them to sleep on. Some people sat on them to sleep, while others lay down. The women usually slept on the lowest bunk with the youngest child. The father slept on the next bunk above with the next youngest sibling. On the top bunks the older girls or boys slept. In the winter the top bunks were preferred because it was always warmer there.

Sleep was not easy. Can you imagine up to a hundred people sleeping in one open room? There was usually snoring, grunting, coughing, hacking, babies crying, people arguing, old people talking or singing to themselves, and dogs barking or scratching. People would get up to rekindle the fires or crawl over things to get outside to relieve themselves. Do you wonder that the Indian preferred to be outside when possible?

I might also mention the smells of past meals, burnt flesh of animals, grease burning, wood smoldering and young children and babies not housebroken and using their beds as toilets. We were indeed a hardy lot.

Each family had a section of the longhouse to themselves. Whenever we needed more room, the end of the building was knocked out and extended. Mostly the people in a house were closely related to each other, and as many as seventy-five to one hundred lived together.

We were usually the same clan in each house and the ones nearby. Ours was the Bear clan. Food was hung from the poles and ceiling, and some was stored in jars on or under the bunks. We kept firewood under the lowest bunk.

We were not tidy housekeepers. Sometimes the women folk would sweep the floor with a cedar branch, but if you did this often you would, over a time, remove loose soil and your floor would be lower than your neighbor's. Then, the first time it rained, your floor would be a puddle of water with your neighbor's garbage floating around in it. So you learned not to be too diligent in your housework. Besides, you could raise the anger of the other women by setting a poor example.

We preferred to be outside most of the time and only sought shelter in the winter time or from the rain. There was little privacy in the longhouse, and sex education was not needed in the young Indian's training. He or she soon learned what mommy and daddy were up to in the light of the flickering firelight. Of course, the lack of clothing on children made them aware of the difference between boy and girl.

These were the sounds and smells of my childhood, and they bring back memories of the people I loved. They were not hardships, but a way of life.

The fire pit was the focal point of the family. Here we cooked our meals and kept warm in winter. Many ceremonies were held by the fire. Many stories were told by old people, men and women alike.

If you had already heard the story at one fire pit you went over to another one. You were welcome between families as if they were your own. Some old tales were very popular. When new ones were told by a special storyteller, all the people would gather to listen spellbound. Storytellers were very well-thought-of and in great demand between lodges. They wiled away many a long winter day and night.

Sitting or sleeping by a fire pit was not the only thing we did in the winter. Long hours were spent gathering firewood, mostly by the younger children and the wives or older people. Many times a woman had to look for moss under the snow to patch the logs near her bed because her child had pushed a hole out between the logs, letting in the cold air by her back at night. When food got scarce in a longer-than-usual winter, we had to look for roots and other plants beneath the snow. Sometimes the snow was very deep in places. The men would hunt for food too. The ideal time would be in a blowing snow storm because, knowing where the deer were feeding on low branches of the cedar trees, we could sneak up on them against the blowing snow as they clumped together with their heads to the wind. We could get close enough in the deep snow, when the deer were handicapped by it, and kill one or two. This would feed the whole lodge for a day or two.

All the food belonged to everyone. No one went hungry. During the summer the women put aside large quantities of corn, squash, nuts, berries and edible roots for the winter. Most foods were dried and put into large, stone-lined pits dug into the ground.

They were usually dug into a hillside on the north side and covered with branches and leaves. They were kept close to camp so animals could be kept away. Sometimes a dog was tied to a nearby tree to scare animals away and to sound an alarm if any came near.

In very lean times I have had to break the ice among the

bulrushes to get to their roots and small shoots for something to eat. I can remember when we used to gather hickory and beechnuts in the fall along with acorns and berries of all kinds. Berries, venison and fish were dried for the winter. Corn was hung in sheaves in the lodge where it dried for winter use. The women tended the gardens with younger children and men too old to hunt. The younger men hunted or made tools and canoes. With this many people living together it was hard to get enough food nearby so the men went further afield to hunt.

As soon as spring came the whole camp changed. With the new vegetation came many foods we had not had all winter. The camp was busy gathering the maple sap to make syrup and sugar. This was a very special time in our year. There were ceremonies for one thing or another every day. The men hunted small animals like beaver and muskrat for the fur and food. The meat was happy change, as meat had a different flavor in the spring when the animals were eating fresh and new vegetation.

Spring was not all happiness. Now we had to take care of those who had died during the winter and could not be buried or taken care of by certain rituals. Some of the clans cremated their dead. Others placed them in baskets in the fetal position and buried them in a shallow grave sitting up, and these had a very nice ceremony attached to them. The most strange one was practiced by a group not far away but still part of our people. They saved their dead until a certain time when they could gather at a sacred village and they buried everyone in a common grave. As many as fifteen hundred or more could be buried this way in a pit twenty feet across and eight feet deep. A pole would be erected near the pit, and certain objects of the departed would be attached to it. Most of the dead were very old or very young.

Not all the time during these gatherings was devoted to the dead. The women had a chance to trade gossip and renew old friendships. The men had a chance to talk and exchange new tools and hunting information. The Shamans had a chance to compare notes and exchange herbs and formulas. They elected new chiefs and subchiefs to replace the ones who had died. They also held ceremonies to bring young men into manhood and give them names. The families arranged marriages and also had a chance to trade off their old or surplus goods. Altogether it was like a country fair.

As the warming weather continued they started to fish in the spring runs and dry the fish for the next winter's food supply. Gardens had to be planted with beans, squash and corn.

Repairs were going on continually to equipment and buildings. Men were constantly making new weapons and tools. They went on longer hunting trips now, and sometimes whole families would be gone for months. Often older men and women and the youngest children were all that were left in the village.

How We Lived

Old people had a special and honored place in our village. Their skills were put to good use. The old men would teach flint tool making, bow making, and snowshoe making. Each had a skill of some kind that he excelled in. The old women would tend the fires; cook and take care of the children; teach girls to sew; make clothing, baskets, and shoes; and do beadwork. In the winter older people always slept by the fire in an honored place. No one ever argued or spoke unkindly to the old people.

There were no orphans or unwanted children in our village. All children were the responsibility of the whole tribe. They could come and go to any family anytime and all were loved and cared for. We realized that children meant survival of our clan. They were our most valued possession. They were always well-behaved. A man's wealth was measured by the size of his family, and we believed there was safety in numbers.

Snowshoes were made by taking a willow branch about an inch thick, removing the bark, and soaking it in hot water for at least two days. It would then be bent in a loop the proper size and tied together at the ends. Then strips of wet rawhide would be fed across the circle and the ends fastened tightly until the whole thing was webbed.

A small hole was left in the center to allow the toe to go through. After they were well soaked with beaver or bear oil, they were hung to dry. These were made in our village by an old man who was an expert. His shoes were so well made and balanced that they were in great demand.

Pottery for bowls, pots and pipes were made by the women who each had her own supply of clay. They were very jealous of their work and each woman had her own way of making her pottery. It was all formed by hand and decorated by the accepted designs in use at that time. Pipes were made by rolling clay around a reed or grass stem with one end larger than the other. This was then bent upwards to make the bowl. Some pipes had decoration on them, some not, depending on what ceremony they were to be used for. Some had deep bowls, some had shallow. Some were formed in the shape of human faces or figures; some were shaped like animals. Pipes were a very personal item and made big medicine. We grew some tobacco but we mostly had to trade with our cousins to the south for a good supply. We also smoked other vegetation on ceremonial occasions. The best pipes in effigy were made by our cousins to the south over the big lake.

Most tools were made by the men. Projectile points and knives were chipped from flint for which we all had our own supply places. Some had a harder flint than others. When I was young it was an honor to be picked by an elder to go on a trip to help get a supply of anything we required. It got us away and out of the garden and away from the women.

On one particular trip we went to gather flint at a place known only by an old hunter who now spent his days making arrowheads and knives which were in great demand by the younger hunters because of their sharpness and strength. About fifteen of us were with the elder, leaving in the early morning and walking to the northwest until we passed the great bulrush swamp. We camped near a big river, then swam across the next morning.

We walked for three more days until we came to a huge outcrop of granite which hung over a swamp. We camped by this. The next morning the elder followed a set ritual before he took us to a nearby pit. The flint appeared as a seam about eighteen inches wide in the rock and had been uncovered for about twelve feet. We boys labored all day hacking out the flint with whatever we could find that was hard enough. It was inspected by the elder, who threw more than half away. It took us two days to get enough to satisfy him, and by the time we were finished there was not one boy who did not have cuts on his hands or knees.

On our return to camp much was made of our success. Many of us now had cut shoulders from carrying the flint in the leather bags. The elder now took the flint and broke some out to size and shape, then chipped away at it with a hard stone until he had made an arrowhead. It would take him about twenty minutes to make one. No flint was wasted. Even the smallest chips could be made into scrapers or cutting edges.

Our days were always filled with work or play. We had a great capacity to find humor and laughter in everything we did. During the summer the platforms where we slept in the longhouse had to be looked after. Most of the branches had to be changed and the moss renewed. Many times during the winter a platform would break through, dumping the sleepers onto the floor or on the ones below. If a bottom bunk broke it was not too bad, but if it was any of the upper bunks all would end up in a tangle on the floor. This would cause great laughter and merriment throughout the longhouse and people would be a long time settling down again.

A young sibling would bundle up with its mother and, during the night, was often put out onto the floor to go to the bathroom and sometimes would start playing and wander off and end up bundled up with some other woman for the rest of the night. This did not alarm the mother, as she knew it would be safe in the longhouse.

Some of the worst things we had to contend with were mosquitoes and black flies during certain seasons. We did everything to discourage them; the best remedy was smearing our bodies with oil. Relief was also found in the open when the wind was blowing. The Shaman and some women made a mixture that helped. Nearly everywhere in the woods there could be found a small plant with shiny green leaves and red berries that grew close to the ground. You call it wintergreen. The leaves were picked and boiled and crushed to get their oil, and this was mixed with muskrat oil and spread on the skin.

It had a strong smell, but besides helping discourage insects it helped older people afflicted with sore joints. Chewing the leaves also helped freshen the breath and slaked thirst and dry mouth. It also was used to flavor other more disagreeable medicines made by the Shaman.

Some other remedies were made from the oil sacks of the fox, beaver, muskrat, deer, bear and ducks or geese. Even parts of the rabbit were used. Most of the medicine came from roots, bark and flowers of the forest. Some were very poisonous and you really had to know what you were doing. The Shaman knew everything about these things and was available to help everyone. His knowledge of herbs and medicine was kept in his head and so was not much known by the average Indian; however, mothers knew the cures for most common sicknesses. Most people carried certain medicines with them when they were away from the village for any time, although help was usually nearby at any village.

Red Snake

My name is Red Snake now, but when I was born my grandmother gave me the name of Slow Turtle because I was two weeks overdue and my mother was alarmed by my slow approach. I had two older brothers and an older and a younger sister. Altogether my mother bore twelve children but, as was usual in our time, children tended to die young. My father was happy he had three sons. In our clan the title of chief was hereditary, but the three subchiefs were elected by the women of the clan. The Shaman was always selected by his predecessor. He would choose a boy to learn from him and he did not always choose his son.

The four chiefs and the Shaman from each lodge or clan formed the council of the tribe and they elected one of their number to be the head chief. The council settled differences between clans and distributed the garden spaces and other common items, but within the clan it was our own chiefs and Shaman who had to settle disagreements. This kept our dirty linen at home, so to speak.

The Shaman was responsible for the well-being of the tribe. He also arranged the proper ceremonial procedures according to our custom, and he advised the chief on matrimonial matters. When a couple wanted to marry, he had to tell the chief whether their lineage was too close or not. He also advised the chief on those things that were most beneficial for the tribe. He would travel considerably in doing his duties, visiting other tribes and trading medical supplies and information. He was the chief's ears within the tribe, because the women told him everything. He always knew who the real father of the children were.

My father was not a chief or any official; he was just a hunter and warrior. He took good care of his family and worked hard and was well-thought-of. When I was three, a year after my youngest sister was born, it came to pass that there was trouble with the Micmac Tribe by the great river that flows to the ocean. Our other cousins, the Iroquois below the great lakes, asked our help to fight these troublemakers. My father and about three hundred other warriors went to war. He never returned.

Many of the braves who returned told my mother that my father was a very brave man who had died honorably and had been a big help in defeating the enemy and banishing them from the territory forever. This did not do much to comfort my mother for the loss of a husband whom she loved very much.

We then automatically became the family and responsibility of my uncle (my father's brother) and we retained our present quarters in the longhouse. As befitting a family of a dead warrior, we were given much respect by everyone.

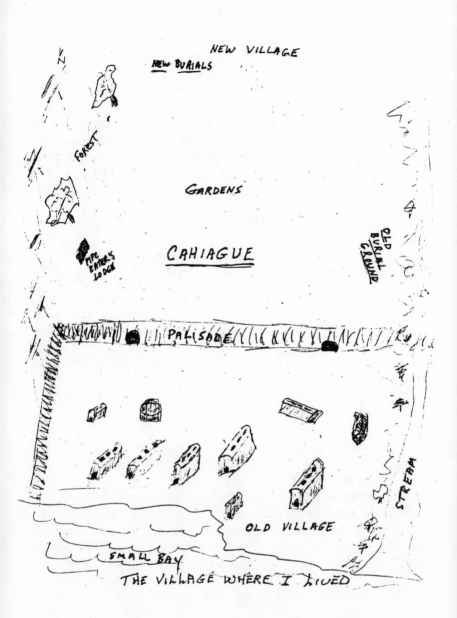

NEW VILLAGE

NEW BURIALS

FOREST

GARDENS

CAHIAGUE

PIPE
EMBER'S
LODGE

OLD
BURIAL
GROUND

PALISADE

STREAM

OLD VILLAGE

SMALL BAY

THE VILLAGE WHERE I LIVED

2. Pipe Eater

When I was young I had the run of the camp and had a carefree time. Everywhere I went I was hugged and caressed by everyone and given good things to eat. When I was five, my uncle took me to a friend of his who was a fisherman and hunter to start my education. They called him Pipe Eater. His name came from the fact that he never took his pipe out of his mouth, even to talk. He would fall asleep with it still clenched between his teeth. He was not always smoking it, but just held it there. His favorite pipe was carved from a kind of stone found not far from our camp, but his usual pipe was made of clay. He went through many clay pipes because he would bite the stem off.

The reason that he was a good fisherman was because he couldn't hunt very well, since his pipe would be smelled miles away. Fish cannot smell the air. He had to fish to eat, but he knew more than most men about how to hunt and was the best fisherman in the village. My uncle felt Pipe Eater was the best choice he could make to teach me to care for myself and to bring me into manhood with the proper skills to survive in a harsh environment.

Pipe Eater was the village character and was well respected. He would not live in the longhouse, but had a small lean-to away from the other buildings. He had a wife and one son, now grown with a family of his own. He told me many stories of his younger days and always had a ready listener. He would not join in on many of the ceremonies and did not believe in all the taboos prevalent in our daily lives.

Once, when he was young, he took a wild creature as a pet, as other children did. His pet was a very large water snake which he kept in a leather pouch. Once, during the night, it got out of the pouch and went to the fire pit beside an old woman and curled up by the warmth to sleep. The woman awoke and, seeing the snake, let out a scream that brought the whole longhouse to her side to see what was the matter. The snake had slithered away into a pile of firewood under the bunk. She told everyone that she had had a vision and a large snake had come and sat beside her and talked to her and told her many things about the future. She kept the people spellbound for the rest of the night, but Pipe Eater knew it was his snake. From that day on he did not believe in these visions. He became what you would call a "part-time believer."

His many pipes were well-known throughout the village, and you always knew when he was about when you could smell them. It had been that which made him not too welcome in the longhouse, even though this smell would hardly be noticed among the many other strong odors there.

I must explain to you how the different tribes were arranged in our district. The Hurons were the older group_or the "People That Smoke." At least that is what the other groups called us. The "Iroquois" name is what the French people were to call us later.

There were only the Hurons at the start in our village, but over the centuries our people moved away and spread and there came to be five different tribes, called the Hurons, Mohawks, Oneidas, Senecas and the Onondaus. They all spoke a common tongue. To the south and west were the Eries, who were related to us but kept to themselves. They grew the best tobacco and traded with us. Further to the north were the Ojibways, who were related to the Algonquins and were a very devious people. Further south, over the big lake, were the Delawares, who were the enemies of all the Huron-speaking people. We were considered village people and stayed in one place all year, while others moved from place to place during different seasons.

Our cousins to the south, the people you call Iroquois, came to our territory during the summer as war parties, and caused us and our neighbors a lot of trouble. We wore more clothes than they did; our hair was left long; and we wore a skin cap on our heads. The Iroquois shaved their heads, except for a small thatch, and wore hardly any clothes. They were ferocious fighters and killed many of our people. Not all were bad, however; only the younger men without older people with them acted this way.

The older people would come to our camps and be made

welcome, as was our custom, and would trade goods and tell us the latest news among their people.

No one bothered us in our village because of the large number of residents. If things become too bad in the outer camps a delegation was sometimes sent to complain to the chiefs and elders of the offending tribe and they would try and keep their young men in check for a while. We also sometimes got complaints about our young people from our neighbors. When a group of us went to favorite areas during the summer to get berries and to fish and hunt, these people would sometimes come to our camp and, after being made welcome to have food and rest, would then make insulting remarks about us. An argument would often develop and soon there would be bloodshed. Then later there would be the matter of revenge, and it would start all over again. There was safety only in numbers. Many times we would find our fishing weirs empty of fish and our traps robbed of animals. They would also take food from our caches stored for the winter. Most people treated each other with respect but, as always, there were some elements that do not respect others among all peoples. There were many small tribes around us with different names, but they were part of our tribe who had broken away.

Contrary to what many white people believe, women were treated with great respect by most members of the tribes. It was a law that they should be. Anyone who did not was an outcast from the rest of the tribe. The women controlled the vote for the elected chiefs and, if they proved to be unsuitable, they voted them out.

So a man wanting to be a chief would take care not to make himself disliked by the women folk. Even in times of war, when captured men were tortured and put to death, women and children were not killed, but were given to other members of the tribe who needed women or had lost a child. Women had charge of the children until they were about five, then they were put out to training by the rest of the tribe. The women had the children for their most formative years, and their influence was felt throughout their lifetime. During this critical period, many children were lost and women who managed to have children survive were well-thought-of. It was sometimes common to see a pregnant woman caring for three others under five years old.

A man who could keep his wife pregnant was well-thought-of also. It has been said by all people that a woman's work is never done, and it was no less so for the Indian woman. Tending the garden, making meals, cleaning clothes and caring for children and the camp and many other chores were her lot. She had more influence on the tribe than most people think. She even helped pick the partners for her sons and daughters for marriage later in life. All marriages were not arranged by parents, but they all did have to be approved by the elders.

Our people knew love as well as your people do. We loved our women and children very much and when they were taken from us we had much sorrow. In fact, men were known to go insane with grief at the loss of a wife or child.

Some couples who fell in love when young were married. Even those who had arranged marriages would eventually become fond of each other in time. We had no old maids or bachelors among our people, nor any unwanted or abused children. We did not abuse or hit our women, as to do so was considered most unmanly. No one made war on women. A man who had a wife who was barren could take another woman to have children. He could not discard the first woman, however, but was expected to care for her as before. Many captive women were given to men also.

Old people were the responsibility of the whole tribe and were kept by their children and were well loved. Some people were driven out of the tribes for not following these rules, and in extreme cases they were killed. If a man murdered another, he was staked to the ground and the dead man was tied down on top of him. He lay like this without food or water for up to six or seven days. After that he had to provide for the man's family for as long as was necessary, and in some cases for the rest of his life.

Many hours of the day were spent playing with other boys. Having battles in the bush was one game we played, much as your children do now. We would choose sides and smear our faces with mud, or the juice of wild berries, and hunt each other down. We would also explore our surrounding bush and, if lucky, would come across an interesting animal. Most boys had some young wild animal as a pet. Some had small turtles, snakes, baby raccoons or birds. Sometimes they had larger animals such as baby deer or bear. They did not keep these too long, as they often became dangerous. I have seen baby porcupine as pets, but they were not too friendly even as babies. Snakes were generally harmless in our area, but there was one we had to watch out for. It was a small rattlesnake about eighteen inches long, usually found near the water and in the rocks. Many people did get bitten by this snake, but not many died. If the Shaman was there he could do much good. As is usual, we boys tried to do all the things the men did. The better hunters or warriors were copied the most. We all had our heroes, even then.

Growing Up

After I began to live with Pipe Eater I had many chores to do. One was to fetch a lighted stick from one of the other campfires. As can be expected, we had to relight our fire when it went out, and when it was cold we would either have to strike a flint or use wood friction to get it going. But if there was another fire going in the camp, I would go and get a fire stick to start ours. On trips away from camp we would light a piece of dried root taken from a tree and it would smolder for a long time. If it started to go out we would suck on the end as one would a pipe and it would burn again. Of course, Pipe Eater also had a fire in his pipe most of the time.

Another chore we had was to gather the small branches used to make fishing weirs. They had to be thin and supple enough to bend easily. They were woven around poles pushed into the mud or sand bottom by the river or estuary on the lake shore. When fish were going upstream to spawn they became trapped in the weir by the thousands, and we would scoop them to the shore where we and the women would later clean them and hang them to dry on racks made nearby for that purpose. In our time the rivers teamed with fish and eels.

It was necessary for us to keep a constant watch on our racks to keep animals away from our drying fish. The raccoon was the worst thief, but sometimes a black bear would come, and the dogs would join us in making much noise to get him to go away. I have slept many nights by the racks guarding them. We also dried animal flesh on these racks for the long winter's eating. It was very important to save enough food for the long winters. I spent many days gathering nuts and berries for this purpose also. The berries were dried in a big clump.

To make us boys behave, our elders threatened us with every kind of demon you can imagine, but the one thing that worked better than anything else was the threat of sending us to the women's house. This was a house about twenty feet square with one fire pit in the center and a hole in the roof. This was where the women went each month to be by themselves. Most of the women who went there were not pregnant, or were young, unmarried girls. They felt that, at the time of their period, they should be isolated from the tribe. This did not mean that they had a rest, for they kept busy sewing and making clothes. A woman who went there too many months was looked down upon because she had not become pregnant, and her husband would be ridiculed by the other men. To threaten to send a boy to this place was a terrible ridicule, and for a man to tell another that he belonged there was the greatest of insults and could end up with bloodshed and much hatred.

It was sometimes thought that certain women went to this house, even when they were first pregnant, because they appreciated the company of their own kind for a while, and it took them away from the constant chores of their hard life. The same was true for the men going on their hunting trips. The trips took them away from camp and the old problems, and let them enjoy the company of other men for a time.

We boys also had to gather firewood and help gather and dry moss. Berry picking was a fun time, and there were many sick stomachs from eating too many. But most of the time was spent gathering.

Both girls and boys had to learn to make the things necessary to survive. The boys made projectile points for both spears and arrows. There were many different types of points—small arrowheads for birds and small animals and barbed for fish spearing. We learned also to make flint knives for skinning animals, scraping skins, and carving wood and bone. We also learned to make lean-tos to sleep in on the trail, handles for tomahawks, and stone tools for grinding other stones and for sharpening bone and flint.

The girls learned how to make the skin clothes we used; how to soften leather to make moccasins for our feet and the leggings we use between our knees and ankles to protect our legs when we walked through the bush. They also made the long dresses they wore themselves along with the beadwork and the fine leather fringe work. They learned to cook many different things, because all we ate had to be cooked a certain way.

Some things had to have the strong wild taste removed or replaced and made palatable by cooking. As is usual, certain women excelled in certain things and became known for their skill, and the work they did was much in demand for trading. A man with such a wife was much envied, and if her daughters learned her skill they were much sought-after.

In a village of some five thousand souls there was bound to be sickness, and sometimes a person became crippled. Most of our illness was caused by food poisoning, sometimes large groups, sometimes individuals. If a whole family ate the same thing they could all be poisoned. At times, younger people would eat some plant or root that was poisonous, not knowing it was. We took great care to teach our children what was edible and what was not, but they would often still try things that smelled nice or looked good but made them sick. We lost many people this way. Other food was just bad, such as meat that was not dried properly or not well enough cooked. Being in a rugged environment, many of our people had accidents, especially children playing in the bush nearby. Some children had arms or legs broken, and for this to happen was very bad. We had no way to reset the bones and they healed as they were. This left twisted legs and arms and caused limping and deformity.

Also, we had many children without an eye. This could happen when playing with bows and arrows. When one was shooting in the air a projectile sometimes hit an eye and blinded the person.

Sometimes both eyes would be affected and they would be totally blind. This could be caused by following someone closely along a trail through the bush and having a branch come back and hit the face. People did not always get hit just in the eyes, but all over their bodies. It was unusual to see a young person without at least some scars. Some of these had amusing side effects. Later in the story you will meet my son who, when he was quite young, was struck with an arrow in the center of his forehead, above and between his eyes. It left a bad wound, and when it healed it left an indented scar that looked like an abandoned eye socket so that he became known as "Three Eyes."

As you can see, we were a very healthy and hardy group. If we lived until we were five, we had a good chance to make it to adulthood. Learning how to live in the wild was the main education for men. Our lives and the lives of our people depended on this; to forage for food near camp was not without danger, but away from the village it was much worse. We learned at a young age that the animals around us were a part of our existence, and much care had to be taken that we did not offend the spirits of these animals or cause them pain. We had to learn to understand all about every living thing in our land, because everything was so much influenced by everything else. If we killed too many of one kind of animal it meant another kind suffered and disappeared, or grew too numerous, and this affected our very lives.

Being A Hunter

When I was eight, Pipe Eater and I went on my first hunting trip, taking along another youth, named Noisy Fingers because he had a habit of bending the joints of his fingers, making a loud, snapping sound. We were to be gone for a few days, the time depending on where the deer were feeding. The trail headed to the east, and we spent the first night by a small lake. It was coming into the warmer weather, so we slept out under a tree. The night sounds soon had us fast asleep, and we knew the new day would bring us to country we had not seen before. At dawn we were up and on our way again, the morning dew and dampness making our feet wet. At mid-afternoon we stopped in a small glade to eat and rest. After a meal of dried venison and some roots, we lay under the trees, and the warm air, heavy with the smell of pine and spruce, put us all to sleep.

Suddenly I awakened to a hand held over my mouth and saw Pipe Eater motioning me to be quiet. Looking to where he pointed I saw a large, black bear about seventy-five yards away, with two cubs running about her. Pipe Eater had already awakened Noisy Fingers and had whispered to us to not move, in the hope that the bear would move the other way. She had not yet picked up our scent, as the wind was blowing toward us. Her smell had awakened Pipe Eater. She kept ambling toward us in a fluid movement peculiar to bears, and when she was about fifty yards away Pipe Eater stood up and shouted at her. I thought he was out of his mind to do this.

The bear grunted and stood up to see us better and Pipe Eater told us to find a tree quickly and climb as fast as we could. I wasted no time trying to find a particular tree but grabbed the first one nearby and swung up into its branches as fast as I could go.

When I was about twenty feet from the ground I looked to see what was happening. Below me was Noisy Fingers in the same tree as I was, and when I stopped climbing he continued on, climbing up over my body to the branches above me, standing on my head and shoulders. After a few curses from me he climbed still higher. Below I heard a great noise as the angry bear tore into our belongings, growling loudly. I wondered if she would try and climb up after us, as I knew she could, but, after eating our food, she and her cubs ambled away into the bush. About an hour later Pipe Eater called us down from the tree and showed us the damage she had done. I asked him first why he had brought her attention to us, and he replied that she was getting too close and by shouting he had let her know we were there. Normally, when a bear sees you it will go around you or go off into the bush, but having cubs made this one protective so she attacked us. He told us that if you surprise any bear too close to you it will attack.

The bear and her cubs had gobbled all our edibles and had thrown our gear all over. Now we had to forage for all our food. We salvaged our clothes and weapons and our small packs with tobacco and Shaman pouches. These pouches contained certain things to protect us and keep us well, and we usually wore them around our necks or hung from our belts.

Sometimes we kept them in our luggage bag when on the trail. I should tell you what we usually wore. The main item was a soft piece of leather, eight inches wide and perhaps thirty inches long, that went over a leather thong or belt around our waist, and through our crotch between our legs, then over the thong on the other side. It was sometimes decorated on the parts that hung down. When it was soft it was comfortable, but when it got wet from sweat or water it hardened and it could rub sores on the inside of our legs and we would have to soften the leather again. We also wore leather leggings, and wore moccasins to protect our feet. We did not wear these clothes all the time, and usually wore none, but in the bush we had to. In the open areas we took them off to make them last longer—especially the moccasins. We sometimes wore a skin cap to hold our hair (which was quite long) from getting caught up on branches. We also wore them for warmth in the winter. We had pouches for our weapons, tools, and food. Traveling was difficult and we had to be as unburdened as possible to leave room for the things we were to carry back to camp.

After our episode with the bear we went on until evening, then Noisy Fingers and I went into the swamp to catch the big bull frogs that were there. When we had enough we removed their back legs and part of the back and ate them for supper. The next morning at dawn we were on our way, after making as many repairs as we could to our gear.

By late afternoon we had covered a good distance, and Pipe Eater decided we should make camp early because we were now in strangers' country. Noisy Fingers and I went off to find something to eat for our evening meal. We were following the shoreline of large swamp or small lake when we smelled a moose ahead of us. We quickly saw that the moose was grazing on underwater weeds near a large patch of bulrushes. Going inland we approached the rushes from upwind so the moose would not get our scent—we were very quiet. Noisy Fingers went ahead into the bulrushes on his hands and knees and I followed closely behind, clutching my arrows in my hand. I soon learned you should never follow another hunter who has been on the trail for a while too closely in this position as it puts your face uncomfortably near his rear end. I dropped back a little to clear my nose and let him go ahead.

About ten feet further he reached the edge of the bulrushes and peered through at the moose, who was still grazing. I came up behind him and, as I did, I heard a familiar sound. Noisy Fingers was snapping his knuckles as he always did when nervous. I was so angry at the fool that I lashed out at his rear end, not realizing I held the arrows in that hand. With a roar like a banshee, Noisy Fingers took off like a bird out into the swamp, landing on his stomach with a great splash. By this time the alarmed moose had given a large grunt and had gone out of sight into the brush. Immediately Noisy Fingers got up and turned toward me. By the look in his eyes I knew I was in trouble. He was about ten and I was eight so I was not anxious to mix with him, but there was no way out of it.

He gave a curse and came for me and we were at it in the bulrushes and in the water a couple of feet deep while I tried to get to solid ground. We fought our way to shore, cursing and grunting with effort. Poking, scratching, kicking, first one on top then the other, we kept on and on and it was far the worst fight I had been in up to that time.

After an hour or so we were exhausted; we lay on the ground catching our breath when we heard a chuckle and looked over to see Pipe Eater sitting under a tree evidently enjoying our fighting. He gave us a few moments to catch our breath then told us to stop playing and hunt for food for our meal. This surprised us as we no longer had any clothes on and there was not a patch of our bodies without a bruise, scrape or cut on it. We were both covered with our own and each other's blood. We finally made our aching bodies pick up our clothes and went on along the swamp edge gathering more bullfrogs since they were numerous and the easiest thing to catch at the time.

When we returned to camp we found Pipe Eater had everything set up and after we had eaten he tended to our wounds. It gave me great satisfaction to see the puncture on Noisy Fingers' rear where I had jabbed him with the arrow. He would have a scar there for the rest of his life and would not likely brag about where he got it. As we sat by the fire afterwards, Noisy Fingers continued to snap his fingers just to annoy me, and soon it even made Pipe Eater mad and he told him to stop.

But after that he never failed to do it near me to annoy me and make me angry. Of course I was always asking him to sit down. Later Pipe Eater was to tell me that he found us fighting and let us go on because it was good to get our antagonism out and over with. He said he could see the resentment of my having a person just a couple of years older trying to give me orders. He thought that we were both winners, aside from the deep gash in Noisy Fingers' rear end. He asked why we had been concerned about the moose, since it was rather too ambitious to try and get it for supper. He said it was a case of our eyes being bigger than our stomachs.

After a rather painful night's sleep we were up at dawn again and on our way. We were now out of our territory and in strangers' land so we could not walk along without fear as we had done before. We had collected some pipe stone and flint at a few places Pipe Eater knew about and had been to a cave where we dug out some red stuff like a red clay. This was used to make a dye very much in demand by our people for decorating their bodies during certain ceremonies. We had a few trade goods with us and hoped to run into some people from another tribe. By midday we were walking along a narrow ridge when Pipe Eater stopped and smelled the air. He asked us to do the same, but we could smell nothing. We used our sense of smell very much more than you use it today. He told us he could smell a fire, so we looked all around but could see nothing.

3. Other People

About two hours later we entered a clearing and suddenly we could all smell a fire. We picked its direction and proceeded along that way. After an hour we came upon a camp by a stream. We stayed back a hundred yards, observing the camp, and could see women and children about. We went slowly toward the camp, and about fifty feet away we stopped and made camp under the eyes of the people there. They showed no sign that they knew we existed but carried on with their work and play. The dogs barked at us for a while and when no notice was paid them they returned to their sleeping.

In the late afternoon we went to within thirty feet of their camp and put down all our weapons before us on the ground, along with a piece of leather with a few gifts on the front of it. Pipe Eater squatted down and motioned us to each side of him. We sat with our legs folded under us, with our backs straight and our hands face up on our knees. We were forced to hold this position until we were accepted. My back soon began to ache and my mouth was very dry from apprehension.

An hour later the men returned to the camp from their hunting and, without even acknowledging that we existed, went abut their usual chores. Afterwards they sat around their fire. Suddenly a young girl approached us with a bowl and, setting it down without a word, she picked up the gifts and went back to her family. One man looked at the gifts as we cleaned out the meager handout in the bowl. The young girl returned, picked up the bowl, and told us her father required us to sit by their fire. This was the way they welcomed us to many fires in this area.

We went and sat down and were fed more than we could eat. All the time Pipe Eater kept telling the man how good the food was and how lucky he was to have a good woman with so many fine sons and pretty daughters. I thought the boys rather sickly and girls ugly. But I guess an old man with an exceptionally stinky pipe and a couple of boys with cuts, scratches, black eyes, looking as if they had been beaten, would be rather hard to accept too. We sat by the fire listening to the men talk until the late hours, when we finally fell asleep.

I awoke once during the night to answer the call of nature after having such a large meal. Before going to sleep again I looked around and two black, shining eyes of a woman met mine, letting me know that someone would not sleep while we were there.

The next morning I awoke to find all my clothes, and those of Pipe Eater and Noisy Fingers, gone. There was no alarm for we knew the women had taken them to clean and repair for us. We quickly got busy and went for food for the camp while the two men sat and talk. We were completely naked, but it did not bother us as this was the usual way then. No shame was shown or expected. We came back with a beaver and a muskrat, which was quickly put into the pot, and we had our morning meal. The tail of the beaver was given to the man, who kindly shared it with Pipe Eater, for this was a much appreciated delicacy.

The boys then took us to an area where there was a big waterfall and showed us the traps below to catch fish. We speared the fish and cleaned them while the girls came and took them to the drying racks nearby. The whole morning was spent like this and it was so much fun. We laughed and talked with each other and they asked us how we came to have so many injuries, and Noisy Fingers told them what happened. They nearly died laughing. By the time we were finished with the story we were laughing too. Noisy fingers even gave a demonstration of his knuckle snapping. Soon everyone was trying it, with some painful results. All in all it was a great morning, and when we returned to camp the elders could see that we were indeed great friends and were happy.

The afternoon was spent lying around and talking with the other boys and girls, who were curious about our families and our village. When we told them how many longhouses there were they would not believe us. Even Pipe Eater had a hard time convincing them, but we asked them to visit us in the future so that they could see for themselves. They knew that such an invitation was not given lightly, and they assured us they would make the trip to see us. In fact they visited us many times later on and we became good friends.

Two days later, when we left them, they begged us to stay on, but we could not. They gave us a piece of leather which had stitching on it in a curious design that would make us welcome anywhere we went in their land. We were to use it many times in the next two weeks, and we were made welcome so whole-heartedly by so many nice people that our hearts were filled with thanksgiving and love for those wonderful, generous people.

These tribes were known to you as the Algonquin. They were very peaceful and hard working. They had been our friends for many centuries and much trade developed, and even marriages between the tribes so that many families became united.

After leaving our friends we continued on away from the direction of our own village and, after a few days, came upon more small family camps like the previous one. They all made us welcome and eventually told us we were approaching their main village, which was about fifty miles away. Following their directions we soon came around to their village. It was beside a small lake and was surrounded by many large gardens. There was a high barricade of poles twenty feet high, pointed on top, surrounding the various buildings, which were not as large as ours. Some were round, and we later found out they were for storage. They had more sweathouses than we did, and these seemed to have more room.

There were about eight hundred people living here when all were home in winter. They seemed to run things differently than we did. They had people doing different things for the whole tribe and not just for themselves. The ones there in the camp had to take care of the gardens and the village repairs while those away were hunting and fishing for the whole group. There were also people away from camp who were gathering fruit, nuts, firewood, clay, flint and pipestone and other things used in everyday living. The people did not use tobacco as much as we did, and many did not smoke at all except on ceremonial occasions. Aside from design, their clothes were similar to ours, but they used more fiber than we did.

We were made welcome and spent many happy hours listening to their stories and gossip. One story was about their ancient ancestors who had been visited by white-skinned people who had come from over the salt-tasting water in large boats, driven by skins hung on racks above the boats. We laughed at this, as we could not see how this could be possible, and all people were our color. How could there be people with no color at all?

They did not become angry at our scorn, but their head Shaman brought from his lodge a large skin bag filled with things we had never seen before. One was a cap made of yellow metal from which, on each side, projected a kind of horn from some great animal we had never seen. Another was a large horn which stood on a metal base, which the old Shaman said was a drinking cup they had used. Another was a large tomahawk head made of hard, black metal, which was very heavy and sharp. The man who used such a weapon was surely very strong. They also showed us yellow metal bands which these people wore around their arms. We were told they dressed in heavy fur skins unlike anything we wore. They told us that these people stayed and lived with them until they died and had taken women and children from their tribe. They had shown their people how to work together and to share works, efforts, and results equally with all.

From the bag the Shaman also took some small beads made of the yellow metal which he said the white people had made from a blue and green stone which he also showed us from the bag.

There were some small bits of the black metal that they had tried to make here also. The black metal was covered with a red powder. The yellow metal turned green when not polished. Many times in my travels I have seen yellow metal, but only in very small pieces which were too soft for any use, though the women sometimes hung them around their necks along with pieces of bone and stone. There were many times I came across a strip of silver metal which was very heavy and so soft we could cut off chunks with our flint knives. Another metal I have seen is a silver color, but very hard, and is usually found only in flakes. We had no use for it in our tribe. The metal shown us by the Shaman had been kept clean and polished. The arm bands were decorated and there were carvings on the drinking cup. The cap had been lined with fur.

We were now beginning to believe our hosts, and to further convince us he had brought forward some people with a much lighter-colored skin than usual whom he claimed were the descendants of these white people. He also had a woman brought forward who opened her cape and showed us she had white skin from her right shoulder down to the ribs under her breast, but I was sure this was only a birth defect. The poor woman was getting embarrassed by the attention, so we thanked her and gave her a small gift for her pains.

I was so amazed by what we had been told and shown that I could not wait to get home and tell this tale around our fire pit.

Of course, we thought there had to be some trickery by our hosts, but they were so sincere we found it hard to doubt them. The items shown us were beyond dispute, but the white skin was not possible. They then told us that some of the white people had red hair. Well, what fools they must be to think that this could be possible. Everyone had black hair! But they proceeded to take from the bag a rolled bark which did contain red hair, and it did look human, but what nonsense; anyone can dye hair red. Pipe Eater took a small part in his hand and wet it, but could not make it black or get any die on his fingers. We knew there had to be some trick involved. They told us that other people with this one had hair of brown and other light colors. Well, this was not believable, but then they actually had some of their people come forward, who did indeed have brownish or light-colored hair. This was something to tell our people on the long winter nights, although we knew we would be laughed out of our village. We spent two weeks there. They told us many stories of their tribe and they were very friendly and good to us.

4. Going Home

By now we had been away from our village for over six weeks and it was time to begin circling back. We said a happy but sad good-bye to our new and generous friends and left early one morning. We walked for hours, then made camp by a river and ate some of the food the village people had given us. For two days we went south over very hilly, rocky terrain. On the fourth day we were walking a ridge when Noisy Fingers' feet slipped out from under him and he went sliding down an incline, landing in a pool of water below.

He had a big splash, came up laughing, then shouted for me to slide down also. I could see that the clay slope rose about forty feet above the water and was wet from a recent rain. I decided to risk it, so I jumped onto my backside and slid down the slope with good speed, hitting the water with a great splash. We quickly climbed up the grassy slope beside the clay, only to slide down again and again with Pipe Eater sitting and watching.

On about our seventh trip we came up over the top, giggling like a pair of silly girls, when we were seized by strong arms and we realized that someone had come up on us in stealth. My heart went to my mouth when I saw them. They had paint on their faces and their hair was shaved off, leaving a small ridge running from their forehead to the back. No one had to tell me they were the feared Iroquois. Two of them had Pipe Eater by the arms while others held us by the hair. One man said, "We do not make war on stupid old men and children. All we want from you is your tobacco and you can keep all your possessions with your lives."

Pipe Eater told them they could have neither and if they would release us and give us our weapons they would surely lose theirs. With this said, one man went to him and hit him on the side of his head with his tomahawk. Pipe Eater fell to

SLIDING DOWN THE MUD BANK TO THE RIVER BELOW.

his knees, and when Noisy Fingers and I saw the blood we went crazy. I grabbed the leg of the man who held me and sank my teeth into it. With a howl he struck me over the head with his fist and raised me above his shoulders, heaving me over the very slope I had been sliding down a few moments before.

I was only partly conscious when I hit the water, but revived immediately and scrambling back up only to have Noisy Fingers collide with me on his way down and knock the wind from my body. We surfaced again in time to see Pipe Eater picked up by four of the Iroquois and thrown over the back to slide down and hit the water beside us. We grabbed him and helped him to shallow water while the men on top laughed and threw stones at us. Both of us boys shouted curses at them until Pipe Eater told us to shut up or we would not live to see our old age.

We waited until we were sure they had gone, then climbed back up the slope. My head ached from the very large lump on it, and Noisy Fingers had a bloody nose and a cut under his eye. Pipe Eater was the worst off with a large gash on the side of his face, and his ear looked like mush. When we had checked everything we found they had taken only Pipe Eater's tobacco pouch. We knew this was one thing Pipe Eater really needed and we wondered what he would do until he could get some more, but he went to his other bag and took out a small pack which he kept aside just in case of such an emergency. We took care of each other's wounds as best we could then had a meal by a warm fire. Noisy Fingers and I went to the top of the ridge and looked down the slope where only a few hours ago we had been having such good fun.

Suddenly Pipe Eater came and stood between us and, putting his arms around our shoulders, pulled our heads to his chest and said to us, "Today I would not have been happier if I had had men with me. You two boys are the bravest young warriors I have ever been with, and your fathers rejoice in their sky lodges for what you have proven this day. I would be proud to have you both as my own sons."

I looked at his face in the dusk and saw a tear of pride caught in the corner of his eye. I did not look at Noisy Fingers, but I knew he also had tears in his eyes, as I did. So came a feeling that happens seldom, between an old man and boys yet to be men.

When we awoke in the morning we ate and went over the events of the previous evening. Perhaps we bragged a little out of foolish bravo, but we all knew that we must be more vigilant from now on, as this is where the enemies of our people made their summer excursions. Packing up, we went on carefully, avoiding the ridges and keeping to the valleys and away from the water's edge as much as possible. About three days later we came into a small glade of tall trees and we were jumped by a group who threw us all to the ground, but thankfully they were our own people. There were twenty-one of them, and by their weapons and dress we knew they were after humans and not animals.

They told us they were tracking a group of Iroquois who had raided a small camp and had skinned the father and stolen all the goods, then left. But they had not harmed the women and children. One of the older girls had run to the village and alarmed the men. They were now on their way, seeking revenge for the outrage, when we crossed their trail. They had suspected who we were because of the smell of Pipe Eater's pipe and had lain in wait for us. The Iroquois may be the best fighters, but our people were the best in the forest. No other had our stealth and knowledge when trailing.

We joined up with them for our own protection. With a group of bloodthirsty Iroquois on the loose, we did not want to be caught alone. It was not likely that they were the same group we had run into because we probably would not be alive today to talk about it. We followed the others at a safe distance, as we did not want to cause any premature warning to the enemy.

We continued along at a slow pace, staying a long way behind the trackers. They left a signal along the trail every so often for our warriors. At nightfall we separated into small groups, keeping about a mile between each camp. This was in case they should backtrack and find us. If we were all in one camp we would all be killed, but this way most of us had a chance to escape if we heard fighting. We knew the Iroquois would leave a small group who would follow the main party to cover their trail and to watch for enemies. After a cold meal—no fires were allowed—we fell asleep as best we could.

The next morning we rejoined the main group and continued following the enemy's trail. By midday I could see our people getting excited, and soon they came upon our trackers who had caught some of the Iroquois off guard and had jumped and killed them. There were only three of them, so we knew they were the rear guard. Our trackers continued on further and so found the main part of the enemy in a small clearing, where they had attacked yet another of our families. The enemy were enjoying the spoils of their forage and were likely to be in this place for the rest of the day.

The trackers returned to our camp and the warriors prepared themselves for battle. They painted their faces and made ready to fight according to custom to insure victory. By the late afternoon they left to meet the enemy. About an hour later we followed, and soon we came near to the camp of the enemy. We could hear their laughing mixed in with the cries of their victims.

Suddenly the air was filled with shouts and noises as our warriors descended on them. We could hear curses, grunts and screams as the men locked in combat. The most sickening sound was that of a tomahawk striking a skull. Once heard it is not easily forgotten. The screams of anguish and pain were now diminishing as we came upon the scene. My eyes were filled with horror as I saw men lying around with their heads split open and with sightless eyes bulging from their sockets. Many were just wounded, but they were the unlucky ones, for the torture that awaited them by our warriors was horrible. Soon they were tied to poles and left for later attention.

We then took stock of our own men and few had died or were hurt, but the surprise attack by our warriors had caught the enemy off guard. The Iroquois had been too busy enjoying their sport with our captured people, who were found in such pain they were dispatched at once by our warriors. There was not much skin left on their bodies and they had been badly cut by the Iroquois. It was not right that they should suffer any more.

We now had an accounting to take care of with the enemy. We got busy gathering wood for fires around the captives tied to the poles. Burning people at the stake was a custom indulged in by all Indian peoples of our times. Our fire was kept in a circle of about two feet away from the victim to make the torture last longer and so they would not die too soon. There were nine fires that night. The screaming of the victims went on into the early morning.

One of the enemy was an old man who was with the Iroquois as a guide, since he had been to our land many times. He told us he had tried to dissuade the younger men but was unable to do so. We did not torture him, but made him endure watching. The morning after we buried all that was left of his people face down so they would have to face the spirits of the underworld. We could give our fallen enemies no greater insult than this. We then turned the old man free and told him to tell his chiefs that we, the Huron people, would no longer welcome them at our village or within our territory unless they could prove to us that they had become peaceful and would do no more harm. He was glad to escape with his life, and we were happy to turn our feet toward our village.

5. Home

It took us three days to get back home. The people had come to meet us miles from camp, having heard of the success of our warriors. No one seemed to notice Noisy Fingers, Pipe Eater or myself, so happy were they as they listened to the stories of the warriors.

We had to be content to sit by Pipe Eater's fire and to tell his son and our immediate relatives of our adventures and of the people and places we had seen during the past two months. But soon even they left to join the rest of the tribe at the big fires, to listen to the warriors and see the things taken from the enemy.

I slept that night in the longhouse with my mother, my two brothers and my two sisters. It was a good sleep because of my mother's cooking and the contentment of being with my people in a warm and familiar place. I spent the next day telling and retelling the stories of my adventures to any who would listen. By evening I could see I was beginning to become a bore. I returned to Pipe Eater's lodge that night because my training was now to begin in earnest. There were to be no more games for me. Had I not been to the most distant lands of the Algonquins; sat around the fires of strange people; hunted deer and other game in a strange land; and brought back strange articles and tools in trade? And most important, I had been with our warriors at a great battle and could talk about it as though I had actually fought with the enemy myself. Now I had a certain stature, and when I walked through the village people whispered about me and I stood straighter, I held my head a little higher, and my chest stuck out like a bird in dance. I was the envy of the other boys, and the girls would look at me a certain way that I found very pleasing.

When a week had gone by, Pipe Eater called to me and told me to take a bowl and bring water from the stream. I was aghast at this. Was not this the work of women? Was he trying to shame me in front of the whole tribe? He stood up and struck me a blow on the side of my head, stooped over and picked up the bowl himself, then went to the stream, filled it and brought it back, and handed it to his smiling woman. He looked me in the eye and said, "All work is for all people, and not one thing is work for one, but for all. When you become a true warrior and a hunter you will realize that even small things beneath your dignity must be done to make you a whole person. How can you be a great warrior or hunter when you cannot carry a bowl of water? Would a great warrior or hunter see an old woman go carry a bowl of water when the water was used for his benefit? There is no place in our camp for a foolish boy to strut around who cannot see his feet for his chest. Go and decide your place in things and return when you have found your reason."

I was so hurt and angry I left without a word and ran to the bush adjoining the stream. Finding a huge clearing with a distant view of the lake, I sat down with my back to a tree to think things out. I thought of the past few days and all that had happened during the summer. I could see that I had been a bit of a bore with my haughty attitude. After all, I had not done any killing and, to be honest, did not really have the stomach for it.

My people were a peaceable, hard-working group, and we did not believe in war, like the people to the south. I then decided that my main goal in life was to become a great hunter and provider for my tribe and family. I would spend my time improving my hunting skills and tools. I slept that night under the tree and felt the next morning that I had never been closer to my surroundings and an understanding what they meant to my people.

I returned to Pipe Eater's camp the next day and sat down at his fire to tell him my decision. He was very pleased and said I would learn much by doing. He now said that we could use a nice fat beaver for the pot on the next day and bid me go and hunt one immediately. I picked up my bow and arrows and tomahawk and, calling Noisy Fingers to join me, made my way to the south of our village where there were many small beaver ponds. We arrived at a good-looking pond, with many beaver runs about its edge, and observed the pond to locate the underwater lodges of our quarry. We found the lodge about in the middle and, though we could not see the beaver, we knew by the recent work done that he was there. We moved over to the dam he had built. It was about five feet tall and thirty feet long. Near the center we broke the dam open, letting out a lot of water and making repairs necessary. I now covered myself completely with mud from the bottom and lay along the top of the dam on the downside.

It was now dusk and soon it turned quite cool. Already I was shaking too much. I wondered how Noisy fingers was doing on the far side of the dam's opening. Soon it was dark and the pond came to life with familiar sounds. About an hour later the moon came out and made it easier to see. Now I heard the slight sound of water splashing and could make out the beaver swimming toward me, with a "V" wake behind him. He approached cautiously from my side and I held my breath for fear he would hear my heart pound. He passed within five feet of where I lay and went directly to the opening. He did not come out of the water to give me a clear shot, but observed the damage to his dam from the water and then swam away. I lay there wondering if he would return. He did return about forty minutes later, and I saw the ripple on the water from a stout stick he was dragging along behind him.

When he got to the dam, the beaver pushed the stick into the damaged place and I wondered if he would leave the water. Suddenly he pulled himself up and proceeded to push at the stick again. I carefully lined his body up with my arrow and pulling back the bowstring let it go. It hit with a plunk and the beaver turned and jumped into the water with my arrow in one side and out the other. He gave a huge splash with his tail and then dived. I thought I had only wounded him and was cursing myself when he came to the surface nearby and, with a little struggle, was quiet.

I jumped into the water and pulled him out and indeed he was a good fat fellow. Since it was now fall he was getting his layer of fat for the winter ahead. That was just fine, because now he would add to ours.

I washed the mud from my body and went to our camp. Noisy Fingers soon joined me and admired my beaver. He said he would wait until daylight and would lie by the beaver runs to see if he had any luck. I started a fire and dried myself off while I cooked a leg of beaver for our supper. With a full belly and the warmth of the fire, I dropped off to sleep at once. Later I awoke to hear Noisy Fingers go off into the night.

As the sun began to warm me up I heard Noisy Fingers returning, and soon he was showing me a fine pair of muskrats. We ate the hind quarters of one for our morning meal. It was late afternoon when we entered Pipe Eater's camp, and he proved more than happy with our catch. He put his wife to preparing our evening meal of beaver. When we were ready to eat, his wife brought him the beaver tail and he divided it evenly, each getting a share. This was an honor, as the tail was usually given to the head of the lodge or to an honored guest. To divide it among us was a great compliment.

After the meal we sat my the fire and told Pipe Eater of our hunt, which he enjoyed as though he had been there himself. After our tale he surprised us by giving both Noisy Fingers and myself each a fine clay pipe and enough tobacco to try them. Noisy Fingers smoked his with great satisfaction, for he had tried tobacco before; but it only made me ill and I had to stop, with Pipe Eater's permission.

The next morning Pipe Eater, Noisy Fingers and I went out to the bush looking for food. We were not really hunting for animals but perhaps some hickory nuts, which were now ready to pick and store for winter. By a large clump of tag alder Pipe Eater bid us stop and told us to remove all our clothing. He would wait on the far side of the brush while we were to sneak up on him through the alder without noise, or disturbing the brush, or scratching our skin. Later we heard his signal and we proceeded to quietly move toward him. I entered the brush sideways, looking for a small animal trail I could follow without disturbing the brush. First I crawled on my knees and then, treading lightly, on my toes. I made my way carefully along, watching every branch and every leaf. For over an hour I crept along, sweat glistening from my body, until finally I came to the far side.

Pleased with myself, I walked over to the granite outcrop where Pipe Eater lay sleeping in the sun. There I made my mistake. Believing that after having made it through the brush there was nothing to concern myself about, I foolishly stepped right on some brittle, dry moss that made a noise. Pipe Eater jumped up and told me what a damn fool I was to make a noise at the end of all my hard work. I should remember that most of the time when you become careless it is because of overconfidence. He told me to study the animals that you have killed and to remember that they became your victim by being overconfident of their ability to escape you. He also said that everything that grows around you is for your use.

What is around you must go into your body to feed you or put on your body to keep you warm or to make and keep you well. All is here for you to take, and you must take care of it, for it is all you have. Because of your need of that which is around you, it is really a part of you. Understand it and appreciate it and it will keep you forever.

He told us that there was not much more he could teach us about hunting, now that we knew how. It was just a matter of practice, and using what we had as well as we knew how. As he felt that we were old enough to contribute to our families' needs, he sent us both home.

6. On My Own

We left Pipe Eater's camp with heavy hearts. I was now nine years old and tall for my age, with a good chest and strong legs. I went to my uncle and mother and told them what Pipe Eater had said. They felt no need to disagree with him as I had already begun to supply their table. I was now more or less left to my own devices and went on a few hunting parties with boys my own age, but I soon found I was most happy when alone. I discussed this one day with Pipe Eater, whom I visited regularly. He said it would be better if I did hunt by myself as it would be more profitable. When boys were together there was often too much foolishness going on, and not all contributed equally to an endeavor but would take their share just the same.

I spent that winter and the next summer hunting and fishing, mostly by myself, and soon learned every nook and cranny within a hundred miles of the village.

I became respected as a good hunter and provider, although I was still learning the ways of the wild. Many times I would be gone for weeks, but it seemed that no one feared for me, as respect grew for my prowess. Many times during the winter I would enter the village with a deer on my shoulder, go to my mother's fire pit, drop the deer, and leave again without saying a word to anyone. I was considered a strange person for not staying to sit by the fire and listen to the latest gossip and stories. I could not stand the heat and smell of the longhouse anymore, nor did I care to listen to stories of their hunting when I now considered myself the best. Even Pipe Eater agreed that I was good.

Many long winter nights I would sit by my own fire, wrapped in furs as the snow blew, the wind moaned over the trees, and the wolves howled a short distance away. My sense of smell was now so keen that any strange odor would make me alert. I was so accustomed to the forest that the slightest change would get my attention, and I now realized that I had become one with it all and was more like an animal than anyone else in my tribe. I knew the animals' habits as well as they. I could identify an animal—its age, sex, and what it was eating—by the look and feel of its stool, and I could tell how long ago it had been dropped. If it was a deer I could tell whether it was female and if it was pregnant. This was important because we never killed a female, especially if it was pregnant or it had young.

I sometimes think that the animals sensed this, because I have come across animals such as raccoons, beaver, muskrats, ground squirrels and groundhogs that had young and were pleased to show them off to me. I have sat quietly by and watched the young animals play together and approach me without fear. I once came across a newborn fawn whom I petted and scratched for over an hour while her mother worried nearby, threatening me by charging and flaying out at me with her hooves, but staying at a safe distance while I played with her child. After hugging its warm little body to me I wiped her off with some sweet fern to cover my odor so her mother would take her back to feed without fear. When I left, the little thing looked after me with such fondness I was tempted to take her home.

I had also learned to look for where the deer had eaten the cedar trees during the winter. Then the next year I could see how deep the snow had been during the past winter by how high up they had eaten. You could also gauge the height of the snow by the height of the rubs made by the deer scratching their heads on the trunks. I also found trees where bears had shredded the bark by standing and scratching, or stretching up and scrapping the trees with their front claws. I had learned to estimate the size and number of bears in the area from such signs.

I was never a religious man, nor did I pay much attention to the many ceremonies held in the village. Pipe Eater never went to the many meetings held and never practiced any ceremony that I was aware of. The Shaman had on many occasions given me items to make medicine on the trail, but I never did the rituals attached to them. The Shaman also gave me many messages he claimed were from the other world, but I never paid much heed to them either.

I must admit, though, that at times in the forest, when the wind was still, I did have the trees speak to me. You may think this foolish, but others have told me they had experienced this too. It was always on a very quiet day, and usually one that was warm. No noise or sound could be heard—not even the crickets or insects buzzing as they usually did on such a day. Suddenly you would hear a whisper in your ear coming from you knew not where. At first you would ignore it; then you would pay attention and listen hard. With our keen sense of hearing, it was possible to get the message. Usually it was to tell you to go to a certain place, and it sometimes brought word from someone passed away. In my case it was always my dead father telling me to do certain things or giving me warnings or advice. I first thought that this could be part of my brain saying these things; however, they did not seem to come from inside my head, but from without. As a boy going on fourteen it still gave me the scares, and at first I would leave that place or give a shout to break the spell.

Once I told the Shaman about this and he gave me another item for my medicine bag. He said I should listen to the voices and not to be afraid, but to heed the advice.

Also, many times I have locked eyes with wild animals and often they have in some way given me a message—or perhaps it is more of an understanding. Once, when I was carrying home a freshly killed deer, I became aware that I was being followed. When I circled back I came face to face with a black bear. We were both surprised and we had a moment when neither of us knew what to do next. He stood up on his back legs and looked at me, and I was about to drop the deer and run, when our eyes locked and I became aware that he was just hungry and meant me no harm. I put the deer down and took out my skinning knife. While the bear sat down about fifteen feet away I slit the deer open and put its insides on the ground. Then I picked up the rest and walked on down the trail. I turned and, looking back, saw the bear eating what I had left with great relish. I made no mistake about getting along the trail as fast as I could, but I would not have been able to outrun that bear if he had chosen to pursue me. I told this story to other hunters and they all had similar stories to tell. It makes me wonder if the Shaman can actually talk to animals as he claims. There were many strange things to learn and this caused me much confusion.

Now that I was near fourteen I began to stay in the camp more and more. Soon my instruction was to begin on things leading up to my being made a man and being named.

This meant spending many long hours with the Shaman and trying to learn the rituals and ceremonies of our tribe. I had to do this, but in a way it was just an excuse to be near the village, as I had suddenly found myself examining the girls a little more closely than before. Oh, I had looked and fooled around before, and when very young I had played with the girls and they with me. But now I was better equipped to play more seriously. When watching the women and young girls washing in the stream I found my breechclout would get too tight from the swelling of my member.

There was one girl in particular who was a captive from the Ottawas, who was about eighteen. She had been given to many men in the tribe, but they could not produce any children by her and had passed her on until they had decided that she was not able to bear. She had ended up with my own mother and was a companion to my younger sister.

I could not understand why she could not bear as she was attractive and had all the right equipment. I started to get excited at the river when she and my sister were there and I swam with them. They could not understand this at first, but soon they became suspicious as to the reason for my reaction. They would giggle and flaunt themselves at me, but I was too inexperienced to understand this. I would stay in the water until after they had gone to give my member a chance to subside, but one day I forgot and went ashore too soon. They shrieked and ran into the shrubs by the shore, laughing as they left. I felt they had laughed at my manhood and did not return for several days.

A week later I returned to the river and was in the water swimming when they joined me. We talked and had great fun and then they left. I went onto the bank and was lying in the sun drying off when I heard footsteps. It was the captive girl, whose name was Still Waters. She sat down beside me and we talked of her people. She reached out and caressed my body and soon I was hers. We mated three times in the next two hours and were both lying exhausted from our efforts when my sister came out and told Still Waters they must return to camp.

For the rest of that summer Still Waters and I were together many times and, although I was only fourteen and she was eighteen, she had experience, which I did not. She showed me many things which I needed to know. I now knew why the hunters did not go away from home for too long at a time, or why they sometimes took their wives with them. I did not get myself a wife until I was over twenty, but I had an active sex life nonetheless. However, it did not become an obsession with me like it did with some of the other boys.

Pipe Eater knew I had been with women. How I did not know, but he knew. He would make much sport of this. I would become embarrassed and he and his woman would laugh at me all the more. Many of the men over the years would make sport of me and ask me how many girls I had mated with, and how many had come with child. Little did they know that the last one had sometimes been their own daughter or captive.

As could be expected, the women outnumbered the men because men were always getting killed in battles or on the trails. The population of women was also increased by captives who were brought back after raiding a village of the enemy. These were sometimes children, both boys and girls. The enemy sometimes were kept also if they showed an inclination to join us. Many times they were a welcome addition to the tribe because of their skills. Nonetheless, they were all treated as equals after they had become accepted. Sometimes the women captives were beaten by the women of the tribe, but most men would not tolerate this and would beat their women if they did not desist.

There was no such thing as an illegitimate child or prostitute in our culture. If a girl had a child it became her father's, who needed all the children he could get as they were his wealth. It was also good as it proved a girl could bear, and this was sought-after by prospective husbands. A woman was expected to remain faithful to her man, but with the men away so often and the whole forest to hide in, it was not hard to meet another without much trouble. This usually happened when the marriage of the woman had been arranged by the family and there was no love between them, although they usually put up with each other for the sake of appearances. When there was real love, and both had a choice, they were usually devoted and did not fool around.

Many marriages were for convenience, as when a man lost his family and wanted to start another. There are always men and women in any group who cannot be happy with one mate and will be unfaithful for any excuse. These are usually very immature people. Sex was not the primary motivating force in our society, but mainly a means of getting children, which is not to say that it wasn't enjoyed, as I have already said. Having food and shelter and children were the driving ambitions and took most of our time.

My education in the tribal lore was still continuing. I heard all the old stories a thousand times in one variation or another. Most of the ceremonies were a variation of these stories. They were told in chants or by dancing to drums. We had orators who talked and talked and talked till I would fall asleep from complete boredom. Some of the songs were nice, if the singers had good voices. An old man croaking a melody was not my idea of entertainment, nor was an old man mumbling past the pipe in his mouth. This seemed to satisfy some of the people, but I had no stomach for it.

I found that all our songs were symbolic, as were the dances. In the ceremony of inducting the new hereditary chiefs, the wampum belt was read. This contained the history of the tribe and was to tell its story from its beginning up to now. I sometimes thought it was more imaginary than fact, but most members accepted it. There was a lot of the supernatural connected with the story which I had trouble believing. The Shaman was supposed to have the power to converse with people from here to fore and hereafter, and could tell your future and your past.

In many cases this was proven to me and I cannot argue against it. In certain ceremonies he said many things to me that only I had known, and I had told to no one. I did not make as much use of the Shaman as I should have, but Pipe Eater had taught me that a man was everything to himself, and no other man was needed to help him. I had proven this to myself, but there was a little part of me that held onto doubt.

We believed in the one Great God, and we called him many names, but mostly Manitou. We also believed in reincarnation and a life after. Living a life of goodness and treating the old and helpless well were our way into the good afterlife. We also had respect for our dead and were careful of the way we treated their remains. Our burial ceremony was the envy of other tribes.

CEREMONIES
BY THE FIREPIT

Manhood

The time of our manhood ceremony drew close and the excitement of the tribe—especially of the parents of the boys—was evident. When the day arrived, we were dressed in our best finery. I had on new moccasins with fancy needle work, decorated leggings of softest deerhide, and my breechclout, which was also decorated front and back with our tribe's logo and my family crest, as it were. My jacket was also soft deerhide and was fringed and sewn with buckskin. I had a new hat made of white mink pelt.

These skins were made from animals I had taken myself. My mother had saved them all for me. They were cured and piled in bundles on the top bunk in the longhouse, and I traded from them when necessary. I was not much of a tool maker and required the very best, so I traded my skins for knives, arrows and tomahawks.

We lined up in front of the great chiefs of the whole village. Our own chiefs were beside them with the old people, and the parents and immediate family beside them. There were over forty boys being named this day. The Shaman gave a long speech, starting at dawn, and then one after another of the Shaman talked. Then the chiefs said their piece, and after that the tribe orator gave his long-winded speech from the wampum belt.

All of it was about was how we should conduct ourselves and how we should honor our tribe, parents, old people, and the dead—in that order. I was starved for some nourishment by now, since we initiates were not allowed to have food or drink until later. They now had a dance to the drums, and we removed our jackets. Then, one by one, we went to the front to be faced by the Shaman and the chiefs. The Shaman came to us with a knife and made our clan's mark on our arm above the elbow, and put on us the rawhide armband that had our family crest or identification on it. It was either one that had been recently made by the initiate's mother or was one that had once belonged to an ancestor.

They then asked who was to name us, and in my case the honor was given to my friend Pipe Eater who, after conferring with my uncle and brother, had decided to call me Red Snake. Later they were to tell me that this name was chosen because I had the ability to glide through the forest unseen and unheard.

After each had been initiated in this fashion, we were told to repeat an oath, taught us by the Shaman, and to make many promises that most of us had no intention of keeping—such as not making war or taking to bed women who were not ours. Mostly it was an oath of moral obligations. We were told to be obedient to the chiefs and the Shaman, which I for one had no intention of doing, because I despised most of the chiefs and the Shaman and had no use for discipline of any kind as I considered myself to be a free spirit. By evening we were ready to eat, and, when we were allowed to, it proved well worth the wait for there was an abundance of food and we ate well.

Afterwards the new initiates had to give a ceremonial dance. During the ceremony, each Shaman had painted on our faces and bodies certain symbolic marks. It made us look like we had on war paint. We danced to the drums for an hour or so, and by that time we were hungry again. Noisy Fingers was named also, and he became known as Winter Hawk.

Why they called him this I don't know. I told him that if I had the choice I would have called him Scar Ass, and he gave me a cuff on the side of the head as we all laughed at him. There was much fun and laughter that night together with comrades. And there was mutual thanksgiving that our initiation would soon be over.

We were now called to the big fire in the middle of the crowd and we sat in a circle.

The great chief lit a ceremonial pipe filled with tobacco and other things and passed it around the circle. Each one of us took a couple of puffs, inhaling the smoke into our lungs. When it was my turn I only pretended to inhale the smoke, so I did not hack and cough like the rest did. The pipe was passed around with much ceremony for over an hour, and I noticed that some of the boys were beginning to giggle and talk too much and too loudly. I felt a little dizzy when I stood up, but kept my balance and dignity, which many others did not.

After the ceremony, the dances and chanting went on all through the night. I could not join in all of them because I now found myself wanting my bed. As soon as it was possible, I left the celebrations and went to my pallet. In the morning I went to the river straight off and had a time getting the paint off my body. The marks made by the knife on my arm had started to scab over so there was not too much pain. I lay and thought of the night and the day before, and realized that there was no need for me to stay at the village as much now.

The only reason I could see for staying nearby was to bed women, but I decided I would have to rely on chance encounters in the forest. Besides, when I returned to the village with food I could always set up a meeting with Still Waters, who by now was my regular partner. I knew I was not the only one in her list of partners, and it was a mutually agreeable arrangement. It was not to last much longer, because she finally became with child, by which partner she never knew, but we all liked to take the credit.

She was finally given to an older man who had lost his whole family in the forest to the enemy while hunting. He treated her fondly and well, and I knew the man to be kind and good. I returned to my forest and stayed for months on end.

During the late spring and early fall I would run into many of my people, along with Algonquins and other small tribes. There were many more Iroquois coming up to our territory than before, and I must admit they did not have as many foolish young braves looking for a fight. We had the odd incident, but not any more than happened with our own exuberant young men. I don't think they meant to do bad things; they sometimes just got carried away with the moment. Some had past experiences on their minds and would become bloodthirsty for a time. Some thought they would be well-thought-of if they committed a great deed against another, stronger group. It was sometimes all the chiefs could do to keep peace between us and our neighbors.

For myself, I kept away from this type of thing. All I wanted was to be left alone in my forest. I was now passing the adolescent period and was coming into adulthood. By the time I was twenty I weighed one hundred and eighty-five pounds and stood six feet tall. I was all muscle because of the way I ate and from living outdoors continually. There was always more to eat than I needed.

Meat was the mainstay of my diet, but many plants and roots were known to me. I loved to feed off the small new shoots from the bulrushes, and a little plant called watercress that was found in cold running streams was my favorite. I would gather this plant and munch it like maple sugar. I became addicted to it and ate it whenever I could get it. I realize now it was because of my heavy meat diet. By craving the watercress my body was telling me to eat more greens. But meat was at times the easiest thing to get and eat.

During the winter, with the deep snow, it was often hard to get anything but meat. If I did not have dried food with me, the craving made me look for any berries still on the balsam trees, or eat the buds from the balsam or spruce trees. This was to prevent a sickness that comes from poor eating. I always tried to have plenty of dried beans, corn and fruit on hand.

Fire

One day in early spring, on my return to the village with meat for my mother's pot, I was greeted by the sight of the village half burned away. Three of the longhouses on the north side had burned to the ground, and another nearby had been scorched. There had been about forty people burned also. As it was still cold, room for the unfortunate families was soon found in other longhouses. I found my own bunk occupied by other people, and all the furs my mother had been keeping for me were being put to good use. I told the people using them that they were a gift and to keep them. I then led a party out to get food, which we brought back in abundance, even for that time of year.

Fire was a constant danger in a longhouse, as our walls were usually very dry and could catch fire easily. Many times I have seen the furs the old people were wrapped in to keep warm catch fire if they got too close to the flames of the fire pit at night. Sometimes children will play with fire and catch themselves or the longhouse on fire, but it was usually out before it could get out of hand. This time it looked as if a container of grease had been put near a fire to melt and was knocked over. The fire caught and spread before anyone could get it under control. Because of the strong winds it soon was beyond containing and also spread to the nearest lodges. Everyone was so busy getting people out with a few meager belongings that the fire simply got out of control. It was fortunate that things were so wet that they were finally able to save any of the village at all.

When people were settled in with their neighbors, the job of cleaning up began. The whole village shifted through the ashes for remains of bodies and collected them together for a burial ceremony in late spring.

They had begun to clean away the debris when I came on the scene. Many of the people had bad burns and some died soon after, but many suffered on and were badly scarred for the rest of their lives. The Shamans used all their knowledge during this period.

The next three months were busy ones, trying to get the longhouses rebuilt and hunting for food to feed everyone. Most of the men stayed in the bush to be near the work of cutting small trees, and the women were busy getting the brush and bark for the walls and roof. It is hard to imagine the amount of clothes, pottery and other normal living things that had to be made to replace what was lost. Of course many personal things were lost forever. This did not happen often, which was a good thing, for it took over a year for things to get back to normal again. You may be surprised to know that even our old enemies, the Iroquois, sent gifts to help out the poor people who had suffered, and we were also helped by many of our close neighbors.

I spent the summer and most of the following winter in the village, most of the time going for short hunting and fishing forays. My mother and my uncle were constantly trying to marry me off to this woman or that. I had no intentions of getting into a binding situation at this time, despite their efforts on my behalf. There were just too many women who were available without the responsibility of marriage. My mother now had many grandchildren by my older brothers and my younger sister. So many, in fact, that I didn't know one from the other. This was not the reason she wanted me to; rather, she did not think I should be alone in the forest so much. They had added about fifteen feet to the longhouse of my clan over the past three years, and it was getting even more crowded and noisy than before.

Once, in the middle of the night, there was a great breaking sound, and I woke up to snow powder flying all over the longhouse. Apparently, part of the roof had collapsed from the weight of the snow, and everyone was showered with it. As it was about twenty below zero, it soon became very cold inside. We could only bundle up with more furs and build up the fires to keep warm until morning. People came from other lodges to see the trouble and stayed to talk. There was not much chance to return to sleep.

In the morning it was obvious that the older part of the structure was rotted, so a new roof was started. This was not the best time for this work, but it was necessary. The snow was about three feet deep in the bush and it was hard to cut the small trees we needed. Everyone in the longhouse went to work and, with the help from other lodges, by darkness we had the roof repaired again. We were all very tired, so we quickly ate our supper and went to bed. But soon people came in from the other lodges and there were story-tellings and much laughter about the snow coming in on the sleepers, and how lucky we were that no one was hurt badly. A few bumped heads and scratches were the extent of the injuries. The families directly under the collapse were given lodging with others until their own area dried out.

From that day on I found myself wandering further and further away from the village on hunting trips, until finally, in the spring, I did not bother to go back at all. I was again at home in the forest where I was most content. Although I had met many new people within the village, I was more comfortable in the woods, where all the animals were predictable and you could count on them to do the same things—not like most people who were changing all the time.

I felt I would never understand men. They help you one moment, then kill one another the next. Their moods change so quickly that often I could not cope with them. I was becoming a recluse in the forest. Although I did enjoy meeting other people in the forest and having long visits with them, I soon tired of it and longed for my privacy.

Pipe Eater Dies

I stayed in the bush until the middle of the last month of summer, when I returned to my mother's lodge with meat. The next day, while we were sitting talking by her fire, I received news that would change my life. A young hunter came to the village to say the Pipe Eater and his woman had been killed in a camp four miles away. Picking up only my tomahawk and wearing only my breechclout, I ran to the camp of Pipe Eater. When I arrived I found him lying by the lean-to with his head bashed in and his woman lying by a large tree with the same wound. I scouted the camp and found that there had been six of the enemy. They had taken everything of value from the camp. Not waiting for the warriors, who I could now hear coming through the bush, I took off on the trail of the six. I followed them for most of the day and found them making camp just before dark. In my rage and grief, and without thinking, I flung myself among them, swinging my tomahawk. I dropped the first two before they knew I was there and, swinging away, I soon had cut the odds in half. When there were but two left I hit one and my tomahawk handle broke. I threw my self at the last one, picking him up and slamming him against a tree, then I grabbed his throat and choked the life from him.

After my head had cleared I looked about me. I had killed all six of them, and I had the head of a tomahawk stuck in my shoulder blade. Apparently, as one had struck at me I had moved forward, and he had struck my shoulder, breaking the handle but burying the head in my flesh. Also, my left ear was hanging down on my neck.

I looked through their belongings and, finding Pipe Eater's things, I set them aside. I was feeling a bit light-headed and sat down by a tree. I was still there when the warriors from my village came up. They stared in disbelief at what I had done. I didn't realize the full meaning of it, as they did, but I was later to understand their amazement at what had happened. Here, in this scene of blood and gore, a man from their tribe— who was known to be a peaceful hunter and who had not been previously engaged in any warlike games or run with young warriors—had single-handedly attacked and killed the most dreaded enemy warriors. To have attacked one was enough, but to have taken on six alone was unbelievable. To find me alive was also amazing.

They came to me, removed the stone from my shoulder, and managed to stick my ear back and cover it. They then packed the hole in my shoulder with moss to stop the bleeding and strapped my arm to my side. They helped me to my feet to walk, but first I picked up Pipe Eater's medicine bag and the bag with his tobacco and pipes. We made our way to the village, where the Shaman and my mother went to work on my shoulder and my other wounds.

The shoulder was very painful now and they redressed it with herbs and moss. They also bound my arm to my chest from the elbow to the shoulder so I could not move it. They even were able to bandage my ear in place.

The next morning I was in much pain, but by now everyone in the village was aware of what I had done and would give me no peace. The chiefs, Shaman, elders, and all who could came to my bed to talk and praise me. I still did not realize what I had done. With the pain of my body and the knowledge of Pipe Eater's death, I was most miserable, and I'm afraid I did not take too kindly to so many people talking to me. Shamans seemed to understand and moved me to their lodge to give me peace and to treat me. The rumors spread around the village of my bravery, and soon you would think I had killed off all the enemy.

When I awoke the next morning I was told that the ceremony for Pipe Eater's burial was underway. I pushed aside the women left to care for me and walked up the hill to the ceremony. This was a long walk up a gradual incline, and it was all I could do to keep from falling—more, I think, from the medicine given me than from the wounds. When I arrived, a low sound was made by the people who parted to let me by. The Shamans and the chiefs were well into the ceremony now, Pipe Eater and his woman were already placed in their baskets, and the ritual of the pipes was beginning. This is where they take the deceased's pipes, fill them with tobacco, and pass them around the circle for each of the conducting leaders of the ceremony to puff on.

When the pipe had gone the complete circle to chants and prayers, it was broken and never used again. I walked to the pile of Pipe Eater's pipes and, without a word, took out the favorite one that he used all the time. It was a plain, grey-colored pipe, with the stem broken off where he had bitten through it. The bowl was grease-stained on each side where he had held it between his fingers. The grease was from countless meals he had eaten before picking up his favorite pipe in greasy hands for his smoke. I took it to the basket containing Pipe Eater and placed the pipe in the cradle made by his crossed arms. The silence was deafening and, as I turned back to the Shamans and the chiefs, I met their eyes and they knew that no one was to dare remove that pipe from the basket. I turned and walked past the people, who were shocked that I had interrupted the ceremony and had flaunted the authority of the Shamans and chiefs. I did not think of it this way, and as I left the people my eyes filled with tears of grief and self-pity for the loss of my dear friend. Most of the village was at the ceremony. They found me later that evening sitting in Pipe Eater's lodge. His son told me that I was welcome to stay there, and that anything I wanted there was mine. I stayed there the night, just sitting in his favorite spot, and in the morning, stiff and cold from my wounds, I made my way to camp. They wanted me to stay again in the Shaman's house, but I refused and stayed with my mother and family.

The next day Pipe Eater's family came to my camp and I gave them all the things I had recovered from the Iroquois who had killed him. I asked if they would want the other things taken from the Iroquois and they refused them. I then had the Shaman destroy everything they had that we had taken. I asked the warriors who had found me after the fight if they had buried the enemy face down as prescribed for a cowardly attacker. They assured me they had—the very next morning and well before we had buried Pipe Eater, as was required. I was now satisfied that all things had been done as per our custom.

The dressing on my arm was being changed every day and was being bathed in hot water with herbs for hours on end. They still kept it tied to my side and I could not move my upper arm. I could exercise the lower part, though not without pain. My biggest worry was whether it would affect my ability to draw a bow again. My ear seemed to be healing back in place, but only time would tell. I stayed with my mother for two weeks and then, with the permission of Pipe Eater's family, I took over his old lodge, partway up the hill by the edge of the forest. I found a certain amount of quiet here and I enjoyed the solitude. My mother had sent my sister to take care of me, but soon she was replaced by a captive woman. From one of the Shamans she had learned much and could also massage my arm. She made me feel good.

The weather had turned cold now, with light snow on the

ground, but many people would still visit me, more to talk about my battle than from concern for my wounds. As I was ill-equipped to survive in my lodge alone, I moved back into the longhouse. All day people would come to my mother's fire to listen to my family and friends tell the story of my killing the enemy single-handedly. The story was told over countless fire pits all that winter, and I could go nowhere where there were no well-wishers and gifts. They continually talked of my bravery until I started to believe it myself, but then I would remember Pipe Eater and his lectures to me, and I would become humble in thought again. My ear was left open to heal now and it didn't look too bad, although it was not pretty. My arm became strong again, but I had to exercise it back to flexibility and worked at it all the time. By early spring I could draw a bow, but not as far as I could before, so I knew it would take time to regain its skill.

Rewards

I soon began my old habit of going away from camp more and more until I was away as much as ten days in a row. My mother and uncle tried to get me to stay at home, because they were afraid that the enemy would try to get me for revenge. Many young men wanted to accompany me, but I refused to let them stand in the shadow of my glory, so to speak. I knew they only wanted the renown that would come from being with me and becoming my companion. I was a loner and intended to stay that way. The forest was my family and my only real friend.

In late spring I returned to my village to see my family, to leave meat and furs for my mother, and to see the games that were due to be played that week. They included wrestling, bow and arrow contests, and spear throwing. Each clan had a champion in each of the events and they were to compete to pick the best in the whole tribe. On the night preceding the final games they usually had a ceremony in which the whole tribe participated. They had arranged a surprise for me of which I had no knowledge.

I had dressed in my best clothes, as was the custom for this ceremony, and when they had gone through the part of it connected to the games they called my name. I went before the whole tribal council, and the great chief in a ceremony presented me with a handsome ceremonial war bonnet. I will describe it for you. The headband was made of fur. Each fur used represented something. The band was made of bear skin, representing my clan. Sewn into it was white mink, meaning stealth; weasel, representing courage over larger animals; and fox for slyness. It had many feathers, and these too meant many things. There were six white eagle feathers with black tips split part way down the shaft, designating the killing of enemies, their number, and the splitting of their skulls. There were black crow feathers, for craft and cunning; and small, colored hummingbird feathers, denoting swiftness and dedication. The tail feathers of a Canadian goose represented leadership. These feathers were arranged in a circle about the headband, and there was a tailpiece reaching to my waist with many other feathers, each with a meaning.

It was an emotional moment for me, and one of pride, because I could see what my people thought of me. My mother and relatives were proud for me also, as were many in my clan.

After the ceremony the village orator told the story of my bravery again, and it was really boring because it had now been told so many times. I felt like telling them the truth—that it had nothing to do with bravery, but was rather the act of a damned fool. My anguish and grief over the loss of my friend Pipe Eater had turned me into a madman, and if I had thought about my actions rationally I would not have done what I did. I was not a very good warrior, and in fact I always avoided killing and raiding other people. I did not like competing, even in the athletic sports of the tribe. After the long-winded speeches, the athletes gave a chant and danced to drums for a while and then we all had a great feast.

The next morning the people again assembled to watch the final games. These ended, the contests and the champions had been chosen and a ceremony was indulged in. During the ceremony the champion would give anyone whose name he called the chance to compete with him once more. The wrestling champion called me and I could not refuse. I did not want to wrestle him, but I had to. We came together in the center of the square and we started. Try as I might, I could not get a grip on him. He was as slippery as a wet fish. When I did grab him he would wriggle out of my grasp with ease.

He finally threw me to the ground and held me there until he was declared the winner. All the people laughed and had much fun at my expense and I joined them. The celebrations covered six or seven days, and I had many long talks with friends and family.

My mother was still trying to arrange a marriage for me, but I would not cooperate. She complained about my goods piling up on the two top bunks in her lodge. I had many furs of all kinds now, and if they were a sign of wealth I would be considered a rich man. Many people had daughters that they wanted me to have, and many were very attractive to me, but I valued my freedom and my forest too much. Unknown to me at the time, this was about to change.

7. Fawn in the Morning by the Clearing

About four days later I was preparing to leave again. I was sitting by my mother's fire pit when there came muffled curses from two fires down. I went down to see what was wrong and was in time to see a woman with a stick hitting a young captive girl about sixteen years old. The girl was not taking it without a fight, and managed to land a clenched fist against the jaw of the bigger and older woman. The woman went flying into a pile of baskets and jars, knocked out cold. We all burst out laughing at the sight of this, and the older woman's man grabbed the girl by her hair and reached for his tomahawk to kill her. I quickly grabbed his wrist and held him by his neck against the pole by the bunks. I told him he was not to hurt the girl as she was only protecting herself, and he cursed me and said if I was so concerned with a captive girl I could take her.

After his anger had cooled, he told me she had been taken a week before on a raiding party near the big lake to our southeast. He said she was a Mohawk and was entirely mad. She could not be reasoned with and was a curse to all who kept her. I looked at her and saw the absolute hate in her eyes. This was one captive that would not be broken. I could admire her courage under her circumstances.

There was something about this girl that attracted me to her. She was very thin, and little taller than most women, and she stood straight, with a proud bearing about her. She was not overly attractive, but she was rather pretty. Her eyes were what got to me. She was like a wild, trapped animal, and the hate in her eyes was evident. I told the man I would like to take her to my mother and asked what he wanted for her. He refused anything and said he was glad to be rid of her. It looked like his woman, who was just beginning to revive, would probably agree. I took her by the arm and she hit me in the face, so I threw her over my shoulder, took her to my mother's fire pit, and threw her on the ground amid the laughter from others in the lodge.

My mother reached for a stick with which to beat her and I told her to desist. I told her that no one was to beat her ever again, and that went for everybody. As she was now my property, this was the way it was to be.

I went to the pile of furs on my bunk and, taking out three white mink pelts, I went to the man and gave them to him. He objected strongly and wondered why I would pay such a high price for the one whom he gladly gave me for nothing. I told him I would not be insulted by a free woman and left.

I then returned and sat by my mother's fire. The girl had watched all that had gone on without moving from where I had dropped her. She had a different look in her eyes now—a sort of puzzlement—but the hatred was still there. I went to the pot by the fire, took her a bowl of food, and sat it on the ground beside her. She looked at it and at me and I smiled. She quickly lashed out with her foot and kicked the bowl over. I just laughed at her and went to my furs and slept. She went to the fire and sat there all night.

In the morning I ate some food and packed my things to go from the village. The girl sat there and watched me and I told her that the top two bunks were mine, and the furs in them. I told her she could make any use of the furs she wished and to keep herself busy, protect my belongings, and respect my mother. I also told her I would return when I had hunted and found the things I wanted. I cautioned my mother and my uncle to see that she came to no harm while I was away. The whole camp knew by now what a fool I had been to take such a useless woman, and to pay such a high price was folly beyond imagination. I had gone from a respected man to one laughed at in one short day.

I went to the forest and found my peace and contentment, away from people again. I visited with people from our village in their summer camps for a few days, and they all were anxious to hear the latest news of the village. But you can bet I never mentioned the episode with the captive woman to them. They told me that there were more Iroquois in the forest now than ever before, though they had not been bothered by them yet. The Iroquois had not been coming to our village as often to trade as they had in the past, and they seemed to keep out of our way as much as possible. Not because they were afraid of us, but to keep peace as much as possible. Things had deteriorated between our people so much that we never bothered to complain to each other's chiefs as we had in the past. It seemed to me that an explosion was about to happen, and it could happen with the least excuse.

I had no hope that they had not heard of what I had done to six of their young warriors and knew that they would like to get their hands on me and would no doubt enjoy skinning me alive. I was not overly concerned about this, as I was confident that, in the forest, none were better than I in keeping out of sight of danger. My senses were keener when I knew danger was around. I did not know at the time that they were not too anxious to tangle with me after hearing all the rumors about me. The rumors got more glamorous in the telling, and many deeds were probably added to the story.

I hunted for a while and returned to my village about three weeks later. When I came out of the forest near the village I was met by the woman I had bought and she handed me a big stick and told me I was to beat her with it. I looked closely at her and saw a black eye and some other lacerations on her face and chest. I took the stick and threw it into the bush and told her that I said she was never to be beaten again and this meant by me as well. I laughed at her and asked why she thought she should be beaten. She glared at me and walked away.

I went on to the lodge and soon found out why. I no sooner got to my mother's fire pit than all the women in the lodge started screaming at me. I finally got from my mother that the girl had fought and argued with every woman in the lodge. Finally, two girls waylaid her outside in the morning and had tried to beat her up, but she fought like a she-bear and had gotten the best of them. I went to the girls to get their story, and what a sorry mess they were. They had patches on their hair pulled out and bite and scratch marks everywhere. One girl even had a piece bitten right out of her arm. It was obvious they had suffered the most, and it was remarkable because both were bigger and older than the captive girl.

I went out and brought the captive woman in and had the Shaman and my mother take care of her wounds. I told her I could see no fault with a person protecting herself and that no harm would come to her. Later that day the clan chiefs called me before them and told me that, for the good of the longhouse, I would have to get rid of the girl. I told them they had just rid themselves of both of us and, returning to my mother's fire, I gathered all my belongings and the girl and moved to the old lodge of my friend Pipe Eater. It had sat vacant since I had last stayed there, and it took a few days to get it in livable condition again. Both the girl and I worked hard, and because of the presence of the girl none came to help us.

We had an understanding after a few days. I would smile at her and she would look at me with hatred. She would not let me touch her, and even when our arms touched accidently she would jump away as though burned. She did not show me any of the work she had done while I was away. But I noticed she had made herself some new clothes, and I could see they were made well and with care. She had a way of doing things that was different from that of our women. Her decorations were new and pleasant to see. The clothes fit in different places. I praised her for her fine work, but she just glared at me as always, and I smiled. Although we slept in the same room by the fire, she slept in the corner, as far away as she could from me. She talked a little now and again, but by no means a lot. She seemed to enjoy talking and seemed to forget herself, but in the middle of a sentence she would suddenly fall silent.

She kept her hair short and neat and almost mannish. As time went on I noticed she did everything to cover her femaleness. She wore her clothes loose so as to hide the shape of her breasts, and when I came upon her suddenly when she was bare to the waist, which was a common thing with our women, she would cover her breasts with her hands and run to cover herself. Even when swimming she went alone to a private place, never near me.

I finally got the idea that she wanted to hide herself from me so I would not get a longing for her and try to mate with her. Perhaps she was shy and I was wrong, but the idea of mating with her had crossed my mind; however, I was not so hard up that I was about to get my hide ripped off for that. I just took to laughing at her and kidding her and telling her she had a shape like a man, which made her very angry, though I couldn't understand why. She worked hard like a man. By this I mean she did things that most women would not do. At times she was good company, and the games we played with one another—you would call one-upmanship—we both enjoyed. We realized by now any other man would have broken her spirit or killed her. I can't explain why I never did, but I suppose it was the wild animal spirit and the raw courage in her that made me not do so.

Many times I would find her in a thoughtful mood and knew she was thinking of her family. One day, when she looked particularly sad, I told her that when we should meet any of her people in the forest I would send her to her family with them.

She looked at me again in a puzzled way and then she asked me about my own family and I told her all she wanted to know. She asked me why I had not married and had my own woman. I told her that I valued my freedom to live in the forest too much, and no woman would live like that because they preferred the life in the village. They might go on the odd hunting trip, but not as much as I wanted to. Besides, I liked the loneliness.

She then asked me why I had paid such a high price for her when I could have gotten her for free. I told her that, at the time, I thought that she was worth it, but since found I had been most foolish. For the first time she smiled and looked at me in the eye without the usual hate, and I must confess that I liked what I saw. I realized that I was getting fond of her. I told her one day that I was going to the forest to hunt and would leave early the next morning. She said nothing and went about her usual chores during the day.

Early the next morning I gathered food and began to pack, ready for leaving. As I turned to take my leave she was standing, waiting for me with a pouch on her back, ready to leave also. I asked where she was going and she replied that she was going with me. I told her she was mistaken and could not go. She asked me the reason why not and I tried to explain that I always hunted alone and wanted to visit some friends. She told me other women went on hunts and she could too. She also said that I had promised her freedom if we were to meet any of her people in the forest. I had no answer for that, so I let her accompany me.

Hunting Together

I went to my mother's lodge to say my good-byes and we left. It was late summer and the leaves were beginning to get their color. The nuts on the trees were ready for picking, as were the late berries. I also had to get some fish dried before the snow came. We were kept busy gathering and drying food for the next month and a half. Both of us seemed to enjoy one another's company, and we had long talks now about many things. She had always addressed me as Huron and I called her woman, so one evening she told me her name. As her grandmother sat outside the lodge where her daughter was giving birth during the night, she saw by the moonlight a mother deer with her fawn, and she called the baby girl Fawn In the Morning By the Clearing. It was shortened to Fawn, and this is what I afterwards called her. She agreed to call me Red Snake, and so we became to be on more friendly terms.

We made several trips back to our lodge—or Pipe Eater's old home, which I now considered mine. Sometimes she returned alone and sometimes I did. Our food supply grew so that we soon had enough to last the winter, though I would still have to hunt for fresh meat. Fawn gathered a large supply of cedar bark which she used to make a cloth. Apparently the Mohawk used bark cloth more than we did.

Now we began to spend more time in our shelter for the winter. I did not mind it as much as I did the longhouse. With just the two of us there was not as much noise or smells of people.

During the winter I spent more time working on my tools and weapons, and Fawn spent most of her days working on furs and leather. She made clothes as necessary, and I was pleased with the designs and decorations she made that were different from ours. She could sew finer and tighter than we did, and so this cut down on openings in our clothes and meant fewer drafts from the cold wind. She would measure my feet continually during moccasins making, and they fit much better. Everything she made she put Mohawk designs on, and this did not please my family, so she started to mix them.

Whenever I went to the clan longhouse I was told that the woman was changing me into thinking like an Iroquois. I laughed at this, but still some of their ideas made sense. They could not understand how a woman could have a gentle name like Fawn and be such a demon. I did not try to explain our relationship and began to spend less time with my people than ever before. I went only when necessary for ceremonial matters.

As soon as spring came I went to the forest more and more, always on the lookout for any enemy who I felt still wanted my hide. Sometimes Fawn was with me, mostly not. I had to be away from her to satisfy my manly urges with a woman. We were not that friendly as yet. She would still avoid me or my touch.

In mid-spring we went a longer-than-usual distance from my village, and I found myself wanting her so much that I began to fantasize on how to get her. I even thought of tying her up, but that is not our way. One evening I come across her bare to the waist and I grabbed her by the hair with my right hand. I held her two arms behind her with my other hand and told her I wished her to have my child in her belly.

When I released her hair to caress her she sank her teeth into my upper arm and I released her with a curse. She went away into the darkness while I sat by the fire cursing in my anger and frustration.

About an hour later she came back and sat opposite me. She sat for a long time, then picked up our medicine bag and tended to the wound in my arm. I would carry the scars of her teeth in my arm forever. She was most tender in her care and, though she still had a look of hate in her eyes, I thought she was sorry in some way. I tried to explain to her that a man had certain urges and if they could be satisfied all was well, but frustration and anger were the result if they were not. I told her I would never take her against her will, but would try again if I thought there would be a chance. She did not answer but sat thinking and said nothing that night or the next day. Finally she told me she wanted to see her family before she committed herself to any man. I was now approaching twenty-two and well past the time a man usually had his own family, but I decided to be as patient as possible.

We went on our way through the forest, heading south to

get to the biggest swamp in our area. This, at one time in our past, had been a shallow lake but was now only a swamp. I knew the Mohawk came to this area in the spring for certain herbs and rushes which grew in large quantities. It was my idea that perhaps we could get close enough for Fawn to call out to them and perhaps find someone she knew to take her to her village and family.

I thought that if she left me she would never return again. I asked her about it but she would not commit herself. We walked for days and kept very close watch for signs of Iroquois. We kept the big lake to our left. I knew the Indians to our right were friendly but kept to themselves.

Attacked

About the fourth day we were walking near a small stream, and Fawn was about twenty feet ahead of me. Suddenly I felt as though someone had given me a hard blow on the back of my left side, and I staggered, put my hand up, and fell against a tree. I looked down and an arrow was sticking out of my side. I shouted a curse to Fawn, who had heard my grunt as I was hit. I heard her say something Mohawk as a blow on my head knocked me unconscious.

I regained my mind and, though confused and in great pain, I realized my head was on Fawn's lap, that there was a fire going, and that it was late afternoon. Fawn was saying something as I drifted into unconsciousness again. When I came to again I could hear Fawn saying, "You crazy Huron, you are going to die if you don't take this." She was trying to force something into my mouth. It tasted warm and bitter. I tried to focus my eyes but they would not behave and I could feel the world turning black again.

The next time I came to it was dark and the fire was still going. In my furs I could feel someone beside me and my confusion deepened. How could I be alive, and who was in my furs with me? The pain in my head was almost unbearable and I groaned aloud.

Immediately the person beside me jumped up and I realized it was Fawn. She spoke to me and again gave me some of the bitter-tasting liquid from the bowl. I tried to speak but the sound was like shouting in a hollow log or cave. It seemed to echo in my head and cause more pain.

For the next week I was in and out of darkness, and the pain was with me more now that I awakened more often. The medicine was not the best tasting and I would feign sleep to avoid it. Fawn finally got it into my head that I had been shot in the side with an arrow, and the warrior had swung at my head with his tomahawk, but Fawn's cry to him had made him change the direction of his blow in time to just catch the top of my skull. It had hit me on the side, above my left ear, and had lifted my scalp over to the other side and bared my skull. It must have also hit the skull bone because my head was so sore. Fawn had replaced the flap of skin and hair and had tied my hair together to hold the scalp in place. She then had applied the thickened sap of the pine tree to make it stick. She had mixed in other medicine also to help the healing.

The arrow had been broken off and the shaft drawn out the back. She had packed the hole with dried moss to stop the bleeding and had covered it with bark cloth. She continually soaked this with some vile-smelling medicine. With the help of the Mohawk who had tried to be my executioner, she had found a small cave nearby and had me put inside while she set up camp and kept the fire going.

The Mohawk had kept her supplied with food and had tried to do what they could. They were puzzled that she was attempting to save me. They wanted to take her to her family, but she would not leave me. They had finally given up on her and had left, thinking I was done for anyway.

As the days went by my strength improved, and with Fawn's help I could hobble along for a few yards every day. If I stood alone I would get very dizzy and fall. This would start my bleeding again and Fawn would get very angry and call me names, none of which I liked. I told her that when I was strong enough I would give her the beating she deserved. Soon I could walk further and my side was healing very well. My head was getting better, though I kept getting dizzy, and my sight would get funny.

It was now over two months since the attack and we decided that it was time to try to make it to the village. We traveled a little way each day and it was soon easier to make a little more mileage. This went on for days and we were happy to make so much progress, but then I got sick again. This time it was in the morning, and I did not feel good but tried to keep going. By midday I was very ill. I was soon in a fever and not in my right mind. Fawn built a fire near me and piled me high with all our furs, but I still shivered with chills. Towards morning I awoke and the fever was gone. Suddenly I realized Fawn was lying beside me naked. This was a shock and I could not understand it. If she was going to do this why not when I could take advantage of it? But I was in no way able to take such advantage, although I would have liked to.

She awoke and, realizing I was also awake, quickly jumped out of the furs. She bent over me to make sure I was alright and left to dress and make some food for our meal. Fawn was very happy that I was well again, but made me stay in the furs for that day. The next day we were breaking camp when she heard some sounds, and soon a group of my people came out of the forest. They were really not prepared to see us there and in our condition. I must have looked terrible. My head was a mess of dried blood and the hair was still tied together and the pine sap and the medicine on it must have looked awful. My side was still covered because it would bleed now and then. My clothes were bloodstained and the grease of many fires was on me. Fawn also had blood on her clothes and also the grease and smoke of our fires.

It was with relief when we greeted them. They soon learned what had happened to us and they were amazed that I had survived and that Fawn had worked to save me and stay with me. They told us that we were still three days away from the village and that they would help us get there. They took over and soon had us on our way.

By the time we reached the village I was feeling better and Fawn had had time to clean our clothes and bathe us. The good food and care from my friends soon had us both feeling better. When at last we were home in our lodge, it was with thanksgiving that we finally relaxed and slept for the first time in the security of our home.

During the next month people would come to our lodge with food and medicine for me to take. Fawn threw most of the medicine away, but was sly enough to keep what she thought to be beneficial for further use. The food was welcome. Our garden had produced well and, after giving our caretaker his share, we still had a good supply. We needed to gather nuts and berries yet for the winter ahead and I managed to help Fawn a little. As my strength returned I would go with another hunter and get fowl and small animals.

The Shaman made regular trips to my lodge to make good medicine and to chase away evil spirits attracted by the fact that Fawn and I were living together the way we were. It did him more good than it did us, but we joked about it and made him feel as though he were doing a great thing. Fawn did believe more in ceremonies and such stuff than I did, and I respected her beliefs and did what I could to help her observe them. These were not very much like our tribe's ceremonies. But it made no difference to me as long as they did her some good.

On long winter nights she would tell me of her family and the way they lived and of their customs. We were a village or a community group. Her people did not live in large bands. Some were in a village of about five hundred people, but mostly they were spread out in small family groups. They would live in camps sometimes many miles apart. They were very friendly to one another and were at each other's beck and call in times of trouble, but still they stayed with their own groups or families.

Some of these groups numbered in the hundreds, while other groups might be as small as ten or fifteen. They always seemed to know who was there and why. They could also quickly gather together to defend themselves. They were more independent than we but could still rely on each other. They were more aggressive than our people, and death was not a great thing among them. And they had more rituals in their ceremonies. They thought more of a man who was a warrior than we did, and the young who fought were more highly thought-of. There were many heroes around, so that competition was a way of life. There was rivalry for the best territory and the best hunting. They had many arguments among themselves and fought one another quite often. In fact, there were many feuds going on all the time, but still they were most ferocious when fighting together against a common enemy.

The winter this year seemed to be longer than usual, though it may have seemed so because I spent more time in the village than before. I did not want to leave Fawn because of the trouble she had with the other women, who seemed determined to be on bad terms with her. I know Fawn did not try to be friendly with them either, and she stayed by our lodge except to get water and firewood. When spring finally arrived I attended the ceremonies without her, as she was not yet really my woman.

I suppose that this was much like when people of your time live together in common law. It was known that I had not mated with her, because I still went into the village for a woman to satisfy myself, and the women were often quite talkative afterwards.

Keeping The Promise

Fawn knew of this, but did not mention it, and I guess she did not mind, as this meant I would not bother her. After the work of spring, and our garden was dug and planted, we left a relative to tend it for us and made plans to leave. We intended to go south, where the big swamp was. This is where we had been when I was wounded. I had decided during the winter that I would go with Fawn to her home village, even if it meant my death. I had had enough of living this way and not having her.

Fawn was now a very well-developed young girl, taller than our women and well-muscled. She wore her hair in braids and wore her clothes well, and she was clean. While our women would always have the same clothes on, she would change often. Most of our men and women dirtied their clothes by wiping their hands on them after eating. Since we ate with our fingers, you can imagine what the clothes looked like. You could always tell what a person had eaten the past year, and how well. Most of the people were very sloppy eaters, too. A child could sometimes find enough to eat from the front of its mother's clothes.

Fawn made me rinse my hands in a bowl of water she kept by our eating plate so that my clothes did not have grease and food on them, and I think it made them easier to clean later. This of course made the other women all the more angry with Fawn, because she kept both of us so clean. They sometimes said we did not eat with clothes on because of it, and many times came to our lodge to see if it were true. We found much laughter in this.

As we were considered strange anyway, it was no bother. Most of the people went to the toilet where nature called them to. They made water anywhere, but sometimes made solids in private. When you approached the village, you were careful where you stepped, especially if you were barefoot, though not all people were so careless. It became a habit to use one particular area. They keep this place away from the water source, and usually well out of the village proper. Fawn and I soon had our place where we did both, as was the custom of her people.

Fawn knew of my concern for my safety around her people and could give me no guarantee that I would be safe, any more than I could her with my people. We now made plans to leave, and many of my people thought I was out of my head to attempt such a thing. Nevertheless, I was determined to go on. We packed our belongings and the next day were on our way. When I picked up my bundle I groaned under its weight. I asked what on earth she had packed and she said just a few gifts for her family. I think she had every fur we owned in that bundle. I found out later that her bundle was very heavy also. I was surely not to be harmed for lack of gifts.

We made our way slowly and without great care, going in a southerly direction. We went past the big swamp again, near where I had been attacked a year ago. We then came to some very high hills which were hard climbing with our packs. Later we came to some rolling country and many small lakes and swamps.

While going along we met many people, some hers and some related to mine. Most were very friendly, and others were happy to see us leave their camp. After many, many days we finally came to a large lake and turned northeast along its shore. Fawn said her people were living on the other side of the lake and we had to go around it.

Many of the people we met told us which way to go around and gave us directions from what they knew. It was not bad country to travel in. The game was not plentiful, but there was enough to keep us supplied. We traded for food when we could to save time. The weather was good and the trails were not too difficult so we made good time. We planned to be in her family's camp before winter.

We were now meeting more of her people, though not of her tribe. They viewed me with great suspicion, and I am sure I would not have lived if Fawn had not spoken on my behalf.

The shoreline was becoming quite rocky and had many inlets and bays to go around, but we still made good time. I was always amazed at the different country and was in awe at the great distance we had covered. The world must be very large place, I reasoned. I had heard many stories about different, far away places and had not believed all of them, but now I was more believing.

The days passed quickly and soon we were in an area where there were many islands offshore. I knew we were near where Fawn said we could cross over to the other side.

Mohawk Country

With some bartering we finally found two of Fawn's people who agreed to take us over. It took the better part of a day to reach the other side. I now felt that I was indeed in a foreign land. My fear intensified as we went south, following a river as we had been instructed. Fawn recognized some of the country as we went along.

On the third day after our crossing over, we met a group of Fawn's people who recognized her. Some were even closely related to her. They made much of her but were cold toward me. She explained that I was taking her home, and that I was responsible for her being alive and well. They could see that she was healthy and well-dressed and loaded down with many goods, so they reasoned that I had indeed treated her well. Even they did not have clothes as fine as hers. They were returning to their campsite near Fawn's family, so they offered to see her home safely. Of course, the rascals expected to be rewarded for this, even if they did not say so. I agreed, as I knew I had no choice. My safety was a little more assured with them along. If we met others they might be curious about me, but would not harm me after finding out why I was here.

It took another four days to reach Fawn's family camp, and there was much joy when we entered. They had all thought her dead and were most happy to see her well and happy. They ignored me the first few hours and I was happy to stay in the background, out of sight. After a while, when Fawn had told the story of her adventures, their attention turned to me. They knew full well that many of their relatives had been killed by my people when Fawn had been taken.

For the present they merely saw that I was fed and given a place to stay which was out of their circle. The celebrations for Fawn's return went on for the rest of the day and most of the night. I was not included in this and stayed by myself, out of sight, in the dark. Fawn was running here and there and I had the feeling she had abandoned me to my fate. I could see there was much love and feeling in her family, and that they were a closeknit bunch. I had no guard to watch me and contemplated making off into the forest but knew I would not survive for long if I did. In the morning I was fed and they brought the bundles that Fawn and I had carried here to my fire. They said not a word to me, but gave me cold looks and hatred, which I expected.

That morning I watched as they put a pole in the middle of the camp and piled firewood near it. "Well, this is it," I reasoned. "They are going to roast my hide alive." Fawn was nowhere in evidence and I presumed she had left me to my doom. It was funny, but I still loved her and could feel no hate toward her. I was getting only what I deserved for being so foolish as to come here.

The Test

At midday the other people of the tribe and some from other camps began to arrive in their ceremonial clothes. I was seized roughly by four men and tied to the post in the middle of the circle. People would walk over and look at me but did not touch me. My bundles were thrown on the ground in front of me. I just looked ahead and decided that if I must die it would be with dignity.

Soon the elders arrived and sat about fifteen feet in front of me. Fawn was nowhere to be seen. I wished she was here to look into her eyes that I might know how she felt about all this. The elders sat for a long time, just staring at me and giving the rest of the people the best viewing positions they could. I by now knew my fate and had accepted it. The chief then said he wished to ask me some questions. I felt like I couldn't care less, and wished it over with.

He said, "Who are you?"

I answered, "You know full well who I am."

And he said, "Yes, but I wish you to say it."

I replied, "I am Red Snake—a Huron of the Bear Tribe."

He said, "Are you an enemy of my people?"

I answered, "As much as you are an enemy of my people."

He asked, "Have you ever killed any of my people?"

I said in reply, "As you, too, have killed my people, and only in anger and not in hate."

He said, "I do not appreciate your replies."

I said, "I do not really like your treatment of me either." I thought he was about to smile, but he kept a stern look. The following conversation went like this:

He: "Why have you come here?"

I: "To bring back your woman."

He: "Do you think we are stupid enough to believe you would do the bidding of a woman?"

I replied, "It was not an act of reason, but of the heart because I wanted this woman to be mine and this is the only way she would agree."

He: "Why did you not just take her?"

I: "Because it is not my way. I am no animal."

He: "Don't you think now that you are without sense? What do you think is going to happen to you now?"

I replied, "You are going to burn me at this stake."

He asked, "And how do you feel about this woman now? Do you still want her when she has led you to this?"

I replied, "I would lie if I were to say I am not disappointed, but I still want her even though my head says I am a fool."

He: "You still want her?"

I: "Yes!"

He: "Did you realize when you came to our country that this might be your fate?"

I replied, "Yes!"

He: "Were you not afraid?"

I: "Yes!"

They sat for a while, staring at me, and then they all got up and went into a lodge nearby. It was now midday, and the sun was directly above and becoming very warm—but not as warm as it was going to be, I thought. I remembered the village and my family that I would see no more. I recalled Pipe Eater and wondered what he thought of the predicament I was now in. I know he would have done what I did, because we were both strong individuals with our own minds.

Again, the elders came to sit in front of me and asked more questions. The chief said, "Did you kill six of our people by yourself?"

I answered "Yes!"

He asked, "If you are such a peaceful man, how did this come about?"

I answered, "They killed my friend—the only father I can remember."

He: "And you killed them in hate?"

I said, "No, in insane anger."

He asked, "Do you not think we should kill you for that?"

I said, "Do you not think I should have killed them for what they did to an old, defenseless man and woman?"

He stared at me for a moment, then asked, "Were you hurt by any of our people recently?"

I: "Yes, last summer."

He: "Then why are you here alive?"

I: "The woman asked for my life and nursed me back to health."

He said, "Then you would say that you and the woman are even—you saved her and she saved you?"

I: "No, because she made a promise to me."

He: "And that was?"

I: "That if I brought her home to you that she would return to my village as my woman."

He: "So you don't think that she promised this to get you to bring her home?"

I replied, "No, because I think she meant her words, as she is that kind."

He: "Why did you save her and become a person ridiculed by your people? You did not know her."

I said, "I saw something I like about her and I admired her spirit."

He: "Is that reason enough to want her as your woman?"

I: "Yes, and the fact that I have come to love her."

There was a ripple of laughter through the crowd, and the elders again returned to their lodge. The people now came near and looked at me closely. None harmed me, but they seemed more curious. I had not yet seen Fawn, but at dusk she passed with a group of women and stopped to look at me.

She said, "Now you will know what pain is, Huron."

I replied, "It cannot be as bad as the pain within me now." She met my eyes and then looked away, but I noticed her chin had tightened as she walked away.

I had no doubt that I would soon die at the stake, but I was not going to die in disgrace. More people were showing up now and they all examined me closely. They put their fingers where the arrows had made a scar, and they looked at my head at the bad scar where the skin flap had healed. On the way here Fawn had cut the last of the tangled hair away and the scar was visible. They also looked at my ear that had nearly been cut off. It had healed, but looked a mess. They did not say anything and did nothing to harm me. Later that night they built a huge fire nearby and they took to dancing and singing most of the night. I was given neither food nor drink and was left to stand with my back to the pole. I sat down, letting my hands slide down the pole, and watched the people.

Escape

I dozed off near morning and awoke later to see that the people had also retired. I began to work the pole back and forth and soon had it loose. I strained to lift it from the ground and finally I felt it move. I was now sweating and my head ached and my arms felt sore, but I continued pulling up. The pole started to fall forward and it was all I could do to lower it slowly. Finally I had it on the ground. I waited to get my strength back, then I squirmed down the pole, pulling my arms from around it. Quickly, I jumped up and made for the forest as fast as my legs would go. After an hour or so of bumping into trees and running into brush I found a fallen tree and lay down to rest. After a while I backed up to a stone outcrop and rubbed the thongs on my wrists until they broke free. I lay for a while in the growing light, thinking what to do next, and fell asleep exhausted.

I awoke as the sun was shining through the leaves of the trees and quickly sat up. My heart jumped because around me were sitting warriors from my host's camp. I realized they had followed me, and now I was once again their prisoner. Their leader said to me, "If you promise to cause us no trouble we will not bind you."

I replied that, given a chance, I would give them all the trouble I could. They jumped on me and bound my arms behind my back. They put a piece of rawhide around my neck and led me along like an animal. When we reached camp we were met with great cheers and I once more was tied to the pole, which had been set in the ground again.

The chief came to me and said, "Do you think you can escape the fate that awaits you today?" They then had food and water brought to me, and an old woman had to feed me like a child. During the day there were many preparations going on and I could see a great feast was being prepared.

At midday there were many people gathering, and I knew my time was running out. The women would look at me and laugh and giggle and the men would just shake their heads. Suddenly, the elders and the Shaman came and sat on the ground in front of me again. They looked at me and the chief stood and said, "By escaping you have not accepted our kind hospitality. Indeed you are a formidable enemy and have much strength. It grieves me to pass a sentence on you, so I have given the one your people have harmed the right to do so."

Fawn came forward then and, taking a knife from the chief, approached me. She raised the knife, looked into my eyes, then reached behind me and cut my bonds. She said, "You are free to go, but you can stay and I will be your woman. We never intended to kill you, but my people insisted on finding out what kind of a man I would take for my own. They have found you lacking in nothing and give their consent. You must first become a member of our tribe, and so a man has agreed to adopt you as his son."

By now I was really confused. She sensed the bewilderment in me and stepped forward and held me close. There was a great cheer from the people, and I was led away to be washed and to prepare for my adoption and entrance to the tribe.

Ceremonies

That evening, dressed in my finest, I was led again before the circle. I was given a pipe to smoke, which was very strong and made me cough, to much laughter. They then began their ceremony, and I met my adopted father for the first time. The ceremony was long and boring. Apparently, my new father was also the village orator and quite long-winded. At last they came to the induction ceremony. If I thought that my new father was long on mouth I was soon made aware that there were others more so. I began to wonder if we were ever going to eat and have something to drink.

Finally, a chief came forward and put a leather thong around my neck. Hanging from it was a round disc with the design of the Mohawk upon it to show I was a member of the tribe.

This did not mean I was no longer a Huron, but was a way in which I could take Fawn as my woman. After this there was much dancing and merriment. Many people came up to me and introduced themselves. They welcomed me into the tribe and into the family of my adopted father. Fawn was nowhere in sight, but I learned later she had watched from concealment and had laughed at my boredom, which she had become able to recognize. I guess I never did get used to ceremonial matters and was not much of a believer in Shamanism. I did realize they had some strange abilities, but kept it from my mind.

After the ceremonies the people sang and danced on into the late hours. I was told that there were to be ceremonies the next day, joining my adopted family and Fawn's, to make Fawn and me husband and wife. After that came the ceremony of the gifts or, to put it plainly, the time when all who could make a claim hold their hands out to get gifts—deserved or otherwise. My adopted father knew he would come into some loot and this is why he agreed to be my father in the first place. The people watched the two bundles lying on the ground where they had been placed when they first tied me to the pole. No one had touched them, as it was bad medicine to do so.

Fawn sent word to me by an old woman that we could meet in the morning before the first ceremony to break the bundles into gift packages for distribution later.

Most of the gifts were furs, so I let her make the decisions. Other things were tools, like arrow heads, knives, scrapers, pieces of flint, and bags of ochre powder, as well some seeds and maple sugar. These were for Fawn's family. If I had known years ago, when I paid two white mink furs for her, that she would later cost me this much, I might have had second thoughts. I was now without goods. It looked like I would leave here with nothing more than the clothes on my back—and a woman to feed and care for besides.

When we met in the morning I had not even been to bed yet. Every time I got up to leave someone would start a speech or song and I would have to sit down again. I smoked more pipes than I ever had before, and for one who did not even own a pipe it made me very dizzy and ill in my stomach. Fawn did not speak but began to separate the gifts. I tried to help but she told me to leave it to her. The gifts she selected for my new father were the worst furs in the pile, and she said they were lucky to get them. The best went to her family and the chiefs and Shaman. When we were finished she put her arms around me and buried her face against my neck, held me for a moment, then left. I made my way to the lodge loaned to me and fell asleep immediately.

It seemed I had just fallen asleep when women came into the lodge, giggling like children, to prepare me for the ceremony. They put on my finest clothes, made by Fawn, and did my hair and put in my feathers.

Then they marked my face with the proper marks to suit the ceremony. They wanted to cut my hair down each side and just leave me with a strip of hair down the center, but I refused to let them. My head scars were bad enough as it was. They made me sit in front of the lodge for over an hour before they came for me. In the meantime I had dozed off again. They made some remarks about how excited I was and hoped I would show more enthusiasm in bed. As they led me to the fire circle the old hags made fun of me, giggling and laughing. They made many lewd and suggestive remarks and questioned my manhood.

After I was seated, Fawn and her family sat down opposite me. Something happened then that I was not prepared for. A small group of people came to the center and faced Fawn's family, and Fawn got up and gave them a bundle of my furs. I knew nothing of these people and wondered why they should get my furs. I was going to ask when I met Fawn's eyes, beseeching me to hold my tongue. I later learned that this was the family whose son Fawn had been promised to when she was a young girl. This was one of those marriages arranged by the family when the children are young, which they sometimes do in our culture. Because Fawn had disappeared they had married the boy to another. But the promise had been made, and the only way that Fawn's family could save face was to buy her out of the contract, which is why they got the bundle of furs.

This had to happen before the actual marriage ceremonies could begin. Everyone cheered my generosity, and I wondered how many more times I would have to pay for this woman. My generosity was wearing thin. I knew that all I had brought here was now gone. What did it matter to me who got what?

Now began the ceremony of the families becoming related through Fawn and me. This was mostly talk, talk, talk by the chiefs, the Shaman, and the family representatives. It went on for about two hours. After that Fawn and I stood before the heads of the families and gave allegiance to them. Then we went to the fire circle again, and Fawn and I gave out the gifts we had prepared that morning. I had to swear to keep her family, and to live with them for a year before we could leave the circle and retire to our lodge. The people kept us in sight, and we returned to the fire after we had changed our clothes to eat and sing and dance for the next hour or so. They were still celebrating when Fawn and I went to our lodge in late afternoon. Women and children followed us from the fire and sat outside our lodge and made remarks.

Fawn And I Are One

We went inside, held each other close, and I whispered in her ear. "Now we are man and mate. If you do not behave you shall get the beating you deserve."

She laughed and said, "You would be foolish to take that chance."

With that I slapped her on her left rear, and it must have hurt, because she became a raging animal and hit me and scratched at me. I grabbed her and we rolled onto the ground and out the door of the lodge. The people outside laughed and followed where we rolled. Fawn was now biting, scratching, kicking and hitting me at will. Finally, through my strength, I managed to grab her and keep her arms pinned down. I carried her off to the forest, with the women and children following us.

I came to a pool of water below a waterfall, which had a

bank about twenty feet high, and threw her in. She hit the water with a splash, and I did not wait to see if she surfaced again but walked back to my lodge. I had sat there for about an hour when Fawn came back and, saying nothing, went into the lodge and changed to dry clothing. Later, without a word, she brought my meal and sat beside me and ate with me. Later I made a fire in the fire pit, and she sat beside me and all was quiet. I felt her hand seek mine and, holding hands, we talked for a while, then retired into the lodge. We were very happy and consummated our marriage, as you would say, that night.

We did not rise until late in the morning. We ate a meal and dressed, then went out to the family circle. As we went along, I walked ahead, as all men were supposed to do, and Fawn walked a few paces behind. I was rather cocky as I walked along. The women we passed giggled, and the men gave me knowing glances and nodded in approval. All of a sudden a bowl of water hit my back, and I turned and saw Fawn with a large bowl and a laugh on her face. She called out "Pompous Duck," then ran.

I gave a curse and took after her, catching her about half a mile away. I threw her over my shoulder and took her to the same pool again and, standing on the bank, tossed her into the water. But this time she grabbed the thong around my neck and, losing my balance, I followed her into the pool. The women and children followed, screaming with laughter. Joining into the spirit of things, they jumped into the pool with us. We spent most of the morning swimming and splashing in the pool and had a joyous time. On our way back to the lodge I heard an old warrior say "He will never tame that one."

I turned to him and said, "I hope not." To which the old women and others cheered their approval.

8. Learning the Mohawk Ways

We did nothing for the next few days, but I soon had to start hunting again. I was not familiar with the area, or their methods of hunting, so I went with a group from Fawn's family to see how they did things. We went for a good distance and met many people who were known to each other. Finally we came to an area that was quite mountainous, with many large trees. Some of the men were put in hiding along a ravine, or in very quiet hollow, and also where a trail was visible that was frequently used by animals. The rest of us made a long detour of about five miles, and began walking toward the ravine, making much noise and talking loudly.

The deer ahead were running away from us, hopefully along the trail where our other hunters waited. By the time we arrived there they had three deer hung and dressed, so we returned to the camp with food and to rest.

My people had also done this type of hunting, but it was only effective when you had enough men to work it out right. The meat was not really enough when it was split among so many. I preferred using fewer people and driving the deer onto a peninsula of land that was surrounded by water. When cornered, the deer would either run back into us or would take to the water. If they did that it was up to the men in the canoes to go after them. With fewer people we usually got more meat. Best of all, I preferred to hunt alone, and I did so after I got to know the area and was known by the people nearby. I never was really accepted by Fawn's people, any more than she was by mine. They never said anything, but I was not treated as one of them in many ways. I worked at hunting and used all my woodland knowledge to bring in more than my share to prove my ability to them.

We spent many nights sitting by a large community fire with Fawn's family, and they told me many things from the past of their tribe. They told me of the white men who had visited their ancestors, and they in turn had passed the story down from generation to generation. The Shaman of the tribe told the most believable story. He told how they had come upon a camp of white people by the large salt water, and that they had a large water craft that was made of trees cut in pieces, joined together. It had a pole in the middle from which was hung a large expanse of skin, tied together, which caught the wind and moved the craft with the speed of the wind. This I could not understand fully, but I did not mention it.

They also had many strange, hard weapons that were very sharp, and one which could cut down trees with a single blow. I told them of the Algonquins that I had visited many years ago and the stories that they told of white people coming to them. It did seem strange to me that my tribe had never had contact with such people. This is perhaps why I doubted their stories, though I did not say so, but still they argued convincingly. They went on to say that their ancestors had finally killed these people from fear and had sunk the big craft. The belongings of the people had disappeared among the tribes, and the Shaman told me of seeing some of these things. I told him I had seen the ones the Algonquin had.

One night, not long after this, they had a celebration for the end of the fall season and for winter's coming. They danced and sang all afternoon, and in the evening, after a meal, they had some competitions. The wresting was quite enjoyable, and I was feeling quite content when I was challenged to a match. I would not have minded, but the one who challenged me was the brave that Fawn had been promised to and who demanded a large sum from me to cancel the agreement. There was not much I could do but accept, because it would be a shame on my people to be thought cowardly.

We met in the circle, dressed only in breechclouts, and grappled with one another. He was tall and strong, but not as heavy as I. We each strained to get a good hold and pushed and pulled at one other. When he rushed me I got a good grip on him and, with his momentum threw him over my back. He landed with a thump, and I knew he had his wind knocked out, so waited for him to regain his breath instead of taking advantage of him.

He finally rose to his feet and approached me. I thought

he would grapple again, but instead he stepped aside, hit me in the eye with his fist, then kicked me in the stomach. I was so surprised at this attack that he was able to strike me a few times before I realized that it was now a free-for-all, anything-goes fight. I thought this cowardly on his part and so did many of the people watching, and they said so. This seemed to make him angrier, and he kicked and scratched and hit out, using both hands as fists. He came at me with such fury that he drove me to my knees, and then I fought back in a rage. In a rage, I hit him in the stomach and drove him back so that I could regain my feet. My one eye was swollen shut and the other was following. My front was covered in my blood and my teeth were loose in the front of my mouth. He came at me with a yell. Taking my time, I brought my hand up from the ground and caught him on the chin with a powerful blow. I could hear the bone of his jaw breaking and could see the teeth come through his lip. I jammed my left hand into his ribs and felt them break. When he started to fall I hit him in the ribs with my other hand and heard still more ribs crack. I then rammed my knee into his face and saw his nose flatten out. I stepped back and took a deep breath, then turned my back on him. I walked from the circle in silence, went to the river and sat down in the water, bathing the blood off my face and body. My eyes were now but slits, and my hand ached from hitting him so hard.

Fawn came into the water beside me and held my head against her breast. I knew she was crying for me.

My rage soon subsided, leaving me spent and weak. Fawn led me back to our lodge, where her women relatives helped her dress my wounds, and gave me broth that soon had me asleep. The next morning my eyes and teeth were in pain, and I realized that the knuckles in my right hand were broken. Fawn was up and soon had me feeling better with her nursing. After a hot broth—because I could not eat hard food—a group of the people came to see me. They said they felt ashamed that one of their tribe would not fight fairly, and that he had not told me he was changing the rules but had taken unfair advantage of me. They told me that he was in very bad shape and would not be around for a while. I told them that I bear no ill toward them or their people and that all would be right again.

They never asked me to be a participant in wrestling again, for which I was grateful. They did treat me with more respect after that, but I had not enjoyed the way I had to earn that respect. Besides the scars in my side, my shoulder, and my head, I now had a hand that looked like a club and scars on my face and chest, not to mention the teeth marks on my arm from Fawn, long ago now. For a peaceful man I was beginning to look more like a warrior who lost a lot of fights.

As winter was now beginning, I spent more time with my new relatives at their camp, and, because my hand was broken, I was excused from hunting for a while. It took most of the winter for my hand to repair itself enough so I could draw a bow again without pain.

I could still set snares for small game and some birds and was able to get some meat for our meals. I longed for my home, familiar surroundings, and my own way of hunting. Although Fawn's family were friendly toward me, I knew I had to be on my guard when I was around the friends of the man I had beaten. They would do nothing near camp, but away from there I had to be careful. This built up a nervous tension in me that made me most irritable at times.

These people kept busy all the time, and when possible kept on the move, going from camp to camp, following game. They were very lithe and handsome. Not many were heavy, and few were fat. My own people were not as busy, and some would get very lazy and fat. These people were clean and washed all the time; mine were not so clean about their surroundings and never washed until necessary. Some of my people never left the village for months on end. They relied on others for fresh meat and other food. The people here were always competing at something and had much fun and ceremonies to do with competition; mine were more religious in their ceremonies.

One morning in early spring, while there was still some snow in patches in shady areas and around trees, the people broke camp, and I learned we were to visit the salt people. These were people who lived by the big salt water. They got their food from the water and made salt in ponds, hollowed out by the shore, letting the water disappear until a white crust was left. We traveled for two weeks to get there and went over some very high and steep hills that seemed to reach to the sky.

The trees were big and close together and in the warm spring days their smell was good. We mostly ate from the land on the way, and Fawn's family met many friends and relatives who made us welcome to their fires and to eat. They gave me curious looks but not much was said about it.

The Salt Water Lake

As we neared the salt water I could smell it in the air a day away. When we arrived there I found it overpowering. The people showed great excitement at our arrival, were most kind about my presence, and treated me as part of the family rather than as a stranger. We sat down by their fire at night and I had my first taste of food from the salt water.

The fish were very salty and dried and took much chewing. The other food came from shells—you would call them oysters. They were very good and I ate quite a few, to my later distress. That night I was very sick to my stomach from eating such rich and unfamiliar food. Fawn showed me no mercy, and in fact was very scornful of my greed. She told me never to eat as much of this food as we would our own, because a little went a long way. She asked me had I not noticed that the others ate sparingly or noticed that the people here were inclined to be a little plump from eating such food just because it was plentiful. I did not eat my fill again while I was in this place because I knew I could not hold it down.

There were more men in this group, because they were not a warlike people. They seemed to be content to fish and gather shellfish and to dry and smoke them for food or for trading.

They also gathered much seaweed for drying and for food. There was no shortage of wood for fires, as it was readily available along the shore. The houses were not very elaborate, just lean-tos made of poles and grass, with some mud and bark. Some of the men did hunt for a change of diet once in a while, but not often, as they usually relied on trading for meat instead. They did not have cold weather and hardly ever had snow, and when they did it did not last. It rained a lot and was always damp. The lodges were built back into the forest from the water's edge because of the continually blowing winds.

I spent a good deal of time here building drying racks,

which were a little different from the ones at home because of the type of fish to be dried. I went back into the forest to get green poles for the drying racks, but we took dead wood from along the shore for burning and for smoking the fish.

The men spent a good deal of time making boats from huge logs. They would use a sharp flint mallet and chisels of stone to hack out the center and make the log hollow, and they would start a fire inside to help clear it out. These boats were about fifteen feet long, with enough room to hold two men comfortable, but usually three went into them. Sometimes the people would decorate them, but usually they were undecorated. They did not paddle too far out into the water with these crafts, but stayed in the shelter of the big bay where they lived.

They had nets made of strong woven grass, and I saw some made of skin and sometimes the intestines of animals. These were weighed down with carved stones, and floats were made of dried wood soaked in fish oil. They would make a large circle towing the net behind their canoes and would come to shore and drag the net in with the help of the whole village. When it was close enough, they would go into the water and throw the fish onto shore. The next few days were spent repairing the nets, which seemed to take quite a beating each time they were used. Much time was spent also lying around, as these people seemed to be able to get what they wanted without too much effort.

It took a certain type of person to be happy with a steady diet of this type of food. Long hours would be spent around the fire pit, telling stories and just talking. It appeared that each family group had a certain area that was theirs alone. This group had exclusive use of this sheltered bay. Most of the good shoreline was taken up, especially the sheltered bays, by different groups, and no one would trespass on the other's area. Sometimes they would cooperate with their neighbors when a particularly large amount of fish were in a certain bay, and they would share the catch. Some had better shallows for the shellfish than others, and they traded between groups. They had a very happy lifestyle.

The people did spend a lot of time swimming in the salt water, but Fawn and I did not like to, as the water seemed to leave a film on our skins, and it felt sticky and uncomfortable.

Instead, we went into the forest where we found a small lake, which fed the stream that passed near the camp and from which they got fresh water for drinking and cooking.

We spent about two months with these people, and one day the family decided to move on back inland, as the weather was getting hot. Fawn's people did not return to their old camp but went more north and east until we came to some very rough mountains and deep valleys. We met many different people on the way, and they were always friendly and curious about me. We finally came to a large lake and we camped there for a few weeks.

Homesick

By this time I was getting impatient to return to my own village, especially because Fawn was newly with a child. I wanted the child to be born in my village, which was our custom, and Fawn and her family agreed. They let me go my way early, as the custom was that I was to stay with her family for a full year to supply food for them all. This was a method the families used to determine if the daughter's new husband was capable of providing a good life for her. Fawn's family never had any doubt about this from the first, by the amount of furs we had brought them for gifts and by my industrious hunting ever since.

So it was with heavy hearts that we left Fawn's family. I had grown fond of her parents, brothers, and sisters and felt I was indeed leaving my own family. Fawn was very quiet and moody for several days but was soon her old self again. We went to the north end of the lake and were to follow a river flowing into it to the other end, where we would find the river we would have to cross by canoe. We hoped we would find the same man that had brought us over the year before.

Before leaving the family we had agreed to meet the following summer by the great rice lake, which was midway between our areas. I had not known of this place, but we intended to pass it on our return to my village so I would learn where it was. We did not hurry, as the country was very friendly. There were many high hills and deep valleys full of large trees. The trails were easy to follow, and many people made us welcome to their fires. They all had stories to tell and would listen politely while we told ours. The people were happy groups and would break into loud laughing at the least excuse. Life was good for them, and, though they had further to go to hunt for game, they were well-fed and happy. The population of all the tribes was increasing, and food was at times a problem. More people were beginning to rely on their gardens than ever before. Despite this, we were always welcomed and given food wherever we went.

We spent a few lazy days by lakes on our way, and finally we came to the large river where we soon found our old friend who took us across to the other side. I was feeling more and more as if I were coming home again. I had never felt this way before, and found it strange to want to see my village again because when there I usually could not wait to leave again. We followed the watercourse upstream and came to the river flowing into it that we had been told about. We then followed this river further upstream. We continued on our way, pausing now and then to visit with people who were camped by the river.

Rice People

Finally, on a late summer night, we came to the great rice lake, which to me looked to be nothing but a big swamp, being shallow across much of its width. We camped by the lake, near the river, and in the morning followed its edge until we came to a camp where, for the first time, we were not made welcome but were greeted with hostile stares. We came to understand that groups of people laid claim to certain sections of the shoreline from which they harvested the wild rice and would defend their parcel to the death, and so strangers were just not to be welcomed. They relied on this crop for most of their food supply, and I could understand their concern at our presence. We explained that we were just passing through and had no interest in their crop.

They let us stay that night by their fires and the next day they were more friendly and told us they would be happy to have us stay awhile. We did so, but only to understand their ways with the harvest. We had places near my village where the women gathered rice, but not in the quantities these people did. Most of the work was done by a man and woman in a canoe. The man would paddle the canoe through the reeds of grain, and the woman would grab the stalks and carefully shake the grain off into the bottom of the canoe. They would be gone all day doing this, and when they came home in the late afternoon they could have the canoe half full of rice.

The other women and children would gather the grain where it was more shallow and would shake the grain into reed baskets. They were always careful to leave some of the rice, in order to have a harvest next year. They knew how to pick it in lines or rows and where not to harvest to keep grain growing for next year's crop. They gathered quite a lot this way and sorted it in large pottery jars and reed baskets after it was dried. We stayed about six days and then, after trading for some of the grain, we made our way around the lake, again following a river upstream.

GATHERING WILD RICE

As we continued north we were told by many people we met that the area we were headed for was very rocky and had many lakes, which made it hard to get around. They told us to always ask directions from the people there. The weather was now turning cool, and the tree leaves were changing colors before falling. I knew we would not be able to make my village before the snow and, as Fawn was with child, it was impossible to hurry. Plans were made to stay at the best possible place we could find for the winter. I knew that the people around this area were distant relatives to both of us, so there were no problems in finding a friendly camp.

We followed the river upstream until we came to a camp where two lakes where joined by a short river that was very rough. I kept out of camp a ways and built a more substantial lodge than I had done for quite a while. It was large, but strong and weatherproof. The bush around us was full of firewood for our fire pit; game seemed plentiful nearby; and fishing was no problem at this time of year.

It was not long before the snow came; however, the weather was not as cold as was common in my village, nor was there as much snow as we had. We settled in for the winter with the knowledge that we would have to leave in the very early spring if we wanted to make my village in time for the pre-birth ceremonies and all the work involved before then.

As there were more open spaces here than near my village, deer were easier to track and kill. The whole place was either lake or swamp and when frozen was easy to travel on. The water stayed open below the rapids and waterfalls, so I could catch the fish which teemed in these waters.

HUNTING DEER

Hearing About The White People

The other people left us on our own and, though friendly, were not bothersome. We spent some evenings around their fire pits, telling stories and listening to theirs, and we joined some of the ceremonies familiar to us. The one story that intrigued me was the one they had heard from some people near the big river to the east of them. It was about a large canoe that was moved by a cloth, hung on poles in the wind. They had visited a small village on the river, and many men had come ashore and stayed. They had traded many strange things for skins, food and fresh water.

The clothes they wore were very fine, and they had moccasins on their feet made of fine leather. The feathers in their hats were from a strange and beautiful bird which none had seen the like of. Strangely, many of the women were given some of these feathers in exchange for mating with these men. This seemed strange to us—that men must pay, or were willing to pay, for this.

Nevertheless, it was said that these men could not be satisfied, but would have two or three women in a night. When the people left in their canoe there was not a feather to be seen on any visitors' hats, but the camp had a lot more color than before. The storyteller also said that some of our people had gone with these strangers in their canoes to see their country. They called their country France, and they were light-skinned and were shorter than we.

A few of them had died after arrival and had been buried nearby the camp. The one bad thing that the storyteller commented on was the awful smell of these people and the strange and terrible smell of their vessel. They were not too clean, and even after bathing they still smelled bad. I did not know whether to believe the story or not, but after all the stories I had heard about these white people I tended to think maybe there was some truth to it, and for some reason this made me apprehensive. Many times I wished I had Pipe Eater nearby so I could discuss these things with him, as he knew so much and was so wise.

The winter seemed to drag on, but I kept hunting, and Fawn was busy making baby clothes. One afternoon, returning to our lodge early, I heard screaming. I saw smoke coming from the camp and, dropping my game, I rushed over. A lodge was burning, and women were restraining a mother who was trying to enter to get her child who was still inside. I rushed into the lodge, snatched the papoose up in its basket, and turned to run out, when the roof came down. I pushed my way through the wall and fell into the snow.

The child was alright, outside of a bit of smoke damage. Most of my hair was burned off, and a burning pole had fallen across my back, making an ugly burn that hurt very much. They helped me to my lodge, and Fawn took her usual job of caring for my wounds. This was going to make an ugly scar across my shoulders, to add to the many I had already gathered.

It was long time before the burn healed, and it made it necessary for me to sleep either on my stomach or sitting up. I could carry nothing on my shoulders for a year after. A week later the whole clan came to my lodge and they were so thankful they made me embarrassed. The little boy I had saved had been given my name in appreciation. This was a very large honor, not given lightly. They later had a ceremony in which I was made the boy's spiritual father, which pleased me very much. They reasoned that I had been sent to their camp by the Great Spirit to save the child and therefore I could be the child's father in the afterworld. As these people were in fact Iroquois, and not Huron, I did not follow their superstitions. Actually, I did not even pay much attention to Huron superstitions.

Fawn and I kept watch on the weather as spring began to show, and, because it was easier to walk over the many swamps while still frozen, we decided to break camp and head for my village. We said our good-byes to our newfound friends and left one cold morning with a light snow falling. Our trip was very tiring and I had to keep close watch on Fawn, as she was showing her child.

We did not hurry, yet soon we were out of the swampy area onto more level ground, sometimes among grassy fields. There were so many camps along our way to stop at night that we always had a warm fire and food. It was the beginning of the growing season, when new leaves were starting to show on the trees, before we came to my village.

9. Homecoming

How happy my family was to find me still alive. And they made much of Fawn, now that we were man and woman and she was with my child. My mother took particular pains to see that Fawn was made welcome and well cared for. The people I knew in the village could not wait for the evening, when they could sit by the fire pit and listen to my adventures since I had left.

After a week or so the Shaman and older women began the ceremonies and rituals involved with the new child's birth, and by the time my son was born all the right things had been done according to our customs. The boy was born exactly fourteen days after our arrival home, so we had just made it and were thankful. A message was sent to Fawn's family by runner, and they would probably know about it within three or four months.

My mother, who now was getting quite old, named my son, as was our custom. This name he would have until he was made an adult and officially named. He now went through many ceremonies in the family, in the clan, and in the tribe. This went on for weeks, as a new addition to the tribe was an event everyone shared. Fawn was up the same day he was born, fussing over him and nursing him. I was very proud my firstborn was a son, and when my mother called him Little Bear, because he had so much hair, I was pleased.

Fawn doted on him so that, at first, I was jealous, but I soon got over it and realized that this was a new relationship within my family. We still lived in Pipe Eater's old lodge, which was now mine forever. I added to it and made many changes that Fawn wanted that her people did, while mine did not. One was to add a small room for storage, instead of piling things on the sleeping bunks. She made many storage jars and kept seeds and what I already had and enlarged my garden, which I detested. I was not a farmer but a hunter. I must admit, Fawn did most of the work in the garden, and I traded meat and furs in exchange for help for her. There were always older or crippled men who would do work for food.

I had now taken my brother's oldest son into my lodge to teach our customs and the ways of the hunter. He was a fine boy and did as I bade him without question. He was good company on the trail and was always laughing at things. When my son was about six months old I took him up the hill to the graves of my own ancestors. I introduced him to the spirits there and asked their good wishes for him.

I sat at Pipe Eater's grave for a long time, thinking of my old friend and how I wished he were here to teach my son as he had me. When I returned, Fawn snatched the child from me and was very angry at my foolish superstitions. But I noticed she did many strange things when she thought I was not looking. We both realized we were raised in different ways, and to bring up our children harmoniously we would have to abide by both our ways. Fawn was now as thin and happy as she was when I first took her home to her family, and she told me she was content.

Not all people accepted Fawn and her ways, but most did not accept me and my aloofness either, so we were usually left alone. Once I was approached by a group of women to stand for our longhouse council but I declined, suggesting they ask my older brother, which they did. I had no use for the politics of the tribe, and in fact hated to be within the village. I was more like the Iroquois—footloose and fancy free, as far as making a home where they wished. My people were community-inclined, whereas Fawn's were always moving about in small groups.

When my child was old enough to be taken to the forest the whole family went, including my brother's oldest son. We did not meet Fawn's family as we had planned that summer, but did the next. During the next five years Fawn and I had four children, but one died at childbirth. This made Fawn unhappy, but she knew I did not blame her. I did feel bad that she had gone through all those months of pregnancy for nothing. It was a common occurrence for babies to die young. I was thankful that the others were still alive and did grow up. We had many happy times together, although the population was rising among our people, and the times were not good.

The hunting was harder, and raiding from other Indians in our territory was more common. Many of our tribe were killed in their camps by outsiders, and many young people were taken away as hostages and prisoners. My brother's son was now a big boy and was on his own more and more. He had turned out to be a fine hunter and went to the forest alone. He was a big help in keeping his family in meat.

My Son

My own son, Little Bear, was soon to be sent to a teacher. He was a little on the chubby side. One day, when he was about four, he was playing with other children in the bush nearby when he was struck in the forehead by an arrow. It was fortunate that it was a small bow, and the arrow was dull, as the arrow just entered the skull between and above his eyes. It knocked him unconscious, and the man who brought him to the village thought him dead. My mother and other women gave him help, and he was comfortable before anyone thought to tell his own mother. When Fawn found out she was very angry and most concerned until she realized the boy had been taken care of as best anyone could do. She had him carried to our lodge, and the other women and the Shaman came to help and stand by. They sent a group of men to look for me, as I was hunting in the forest. They found me the next day, some distance away. When informed of what happened, I dropped everything and ran all the way to the village. It took me six hours to arrive and I was exhausted, but I would not rest until they told me he was alive, though not awake.

I went into the lodge and looked at my son. He had gum plastered on his forehead and was breathing deeply, groaning once in a while. Fawn and my mother were sitting beside him, and two Shamans were mumbling and waving feathers and rattles over him. There was a bowl of evil-smelling, smoking mixture at his head. Three old men were in a corner, softly beating drums while the Shamans sang. I sat beside Fawn, and she took my hand and laid her head on my shoulder. We said nothing, but sat and looked at our son all that night and most of the next day. Finally, the boy groaned aloud and started to cry. He opened his eyes and saw his mother, and she bent over to comfort him. I lay down on a robe in front of the lodge and slept fitfully for a while. When I awoke I went inside to find he had gone to sleep, as had Fawn. The old women sat and kept watch.

I now looked closely at my son for the first time and noticed his eyes were both black and later was to observe that his eyes were bloodshot, and he complained of fuzzy sight. His forehead was so swollen that it was even noticeable under the gum placed over it. Later, when his wounds healed, he had an indentation in his forehead where he had been struck by the arrow that looked like an empty eye socket. Because of this he was called Three Eyes for the rest of his life. I did not care for that name, but it did suit him. At the time I was happy that he had survived and was well again. It meant a lot for a man to have a son to carry on the family.

As he was my only boy, I was most thankful that he survived. This does not mean that I did not love my daughters as much as I loved my son, for I did.

That night Fawn and I lay close together, getting strength from each other. This had also happened just before she had given birth to the child that died, and I wondered if it had any particular meaning. I stayed near the lodge until the boy was up and around again. The men who had found me in the forest had brought in my gear and the meat from the animals I had killed.

They held a thanksgiving ceremony for my son's recovery, and at this time it was necessary for me to show my appreciation to those who had labored on his behalf. This cost me considerably in furs and other goods, but there was no escape. The amount you have showed the value you placed on the life they saved. Besides, the spirits would be most unhappy if you did not show thanks. I did not believe that the Shamans with their drums, rattles, feathers, and chanting did much good, but I wasn't taking any chances. The old women were the best help and I repaid them in many ways, as most were without family. In the future I gave all my surplus meat to them, and they said that I held my son in high esteem to be so generous for so long.

My mother passed over to the evening sky that fall, and it made me most unhappy. Though she and I had not been as close as she had been with my brothers and sisters, I felt I had somehow lost a special contact with an older time.

We did the things necessary to make her trip easier into the great beyond, to sit by my father's fire forever. We made many gifts to the great ones and did the proper ceremonies, as was our custom.

If anything good had happened that year it was that Fawn and I drew even closer to one another. It was not good to build a life together on grief, so we knew we must remember the happy times. And many happy times there were. Our children were a joy to us, and all the more so because we did. not have to share them as others did theirs in the longhouses. There they had the run of the whole building, and all the families were soon looked on as one. This was perhaps good training for communal living, but not what Fawn and I wanted. We liked to keep a little distance away from other people for the sake of peace and quiet.

In the summer we spent many days together, teaching the children to swim and hunt and to gather fruit and nuts for the winter. The boy was soon learning to make hunting tools for himself, and the girls had plenty of animal skins to keep them busy. From their mother they learned to make pottery, and the older women, who were more skilled than Fawn, taught them to make other objects. The girls learned to gather and cook many different foods, from the garden and the forest.

We later had other children who did not survive the first year, and we were saddened by their passing. We also knew we had done the best we could under the harsh environment we had to live in.

If a woman was in the village when the child was born, the baby usually had a better chance because other women helped her. Many women had their babies in a hunting camp and very often were alone. A woman in our time could have a baby and be about her usual chores an hour later. In very cold weather, when they were in a snowbound camp by themselves, women often lost their babies. Hot water was not available to wash the new child, and the mother would fill her mouth with water or even snow to warm it. When it was warm enough she would squirt the water onto the baby to wash it off and would use dried moss to wipe it. This could take some time, and in some cases the baby was not cleaned off for hours. In extreme cold, the mother would put the baby under the front of her garment, between breasts, to feed the baby and keep it warm. She would, under normal circumstances, put the baby into a leather bag with dried moss on the bottom, which she carried on her back. Some were lined with fur and others with a soft wool made from dried cedar bark. The moss at the bottom of the bag would be changed when necessary, as you do with diapers.

Mothers would nurse a baby until it was up to two years of age, and in the longhouses I have seen mothers pick up and nurse other women's babies as though they were their own. In some cases even grandmothers would still have a baby nursing at the same time as their oldest daughters, and they would feed any baby that was handy or that was otherwise being bothersome. Some children did not even know their actual parents in the longhouse until they were older.

We could not understand how a seemingly healthy child would very suddenly sicken and die, when in some cases a crippled or sickly child would live. The Shaman said it was bad spirits, and that the child was not allowed to live for some reason or other. Fawn and I did not really believe this, as most of the children that died had parents that were lazy and did not give the child proper care and food. Many children died from eating poisoned berries and leaves of plants. Others drowned in the lakes and streams nearby. Some fell from trees or over cliffs and were killed. Others were attacked by enemies in camps away from the village. Sometimes children would wander away into the forest, become lost, and would perish before we could find them. I felt the parents were to blame, not the spirits. Pity the poor family who had a father that was always raiding other Indian camps to prove himself and never did, because his family was always hungry. There were groups of men in our village like this, and they stayed together and would be brave only in each other's company.

The hard-working man who hunted and tended his garden was really the bravest of men. He was better thought-of and highly respected. The others were the bums of our society and were the disappointment of our people. Some did eventually grow up and become real men, and their families were then happy. The things they took from the camps they raided were not very well-received. Some women were very lazy. They would go from one man to another and were never happy with one man. They were considered to be ill, and the Shaman would work on them to drive away the evil spirits that possessed them. I think that the Shaman was just having a good time, as he never to my knowledge cured any of them. These women were usually widows or captive women, or ones whose men were very old or away from home too long.

After my mother died the family ties were weakened. I had no reason to go to the longhouse except to attend some important ceremony. Most of my time was spent in the forest, hunting to keep meat on the table. Fawn kept the garden in excellent shape with the help of the two girls. My son went to my oldest brother to learn tribal lore and how to participate in certain ceremonies. His knowledge of hunting and tool-making was left to me, as I was considered one of the best in the tribe.

One year we left him with his grandparents, the Mohawks, who met us at the big swamp lake in the summer and took him to their camp. We met them there again the next summer. He was glad to see us and we him. His grandparents were sad to leave him. He had learned many things, and the most important was to think for himself and to care for himself in the forest. He had spent the whole time away from us hunting and moving from camp to camp, as is the Mohawk ways. He had fished in the salt water and had enjoyed the fish, which were very different from ours.

It took many nights around the fire pit for him to tell us all his adventures and the stories he had heard. One thing that disturbed me was a medicine bag he wore, given him by the Shaman of the Mohawk to protect him, and a medallion worn on a hide cord around his neck that showed him to be of the Beaver tribe of the Mohawk.

The Problem Of Being Huron And Mohawk

I made him take it off, and reminded him that he was a Huron of the Bear tribe. He was soon to have the ceremony that made it legal in our tribe. A son must be of the tribe of his father and can never change tribes.

The medicine bag I did not worry about, but it soon became obvious that our tribe Shaman did not take kindly to it and asked that he remove it. I agreed that he should when in the village, but out of the village he could wear it if he wished. This seemed to please Fawn, who understood our ways too. Fawn made him a charm like one I wore, that showed us to be Huron, but with an allegiance to the tribe of her parents. Though the Shaman and council did not approve of this, I was not to be told what I could or could not wear, and no one was strong enough to force me to change my mind, although my brother, who was on the tribe's council, tried to persuade me not to wear it.

The problems about this were the result of continued hostilities between us and Iroquois tribes, who were now becoming more insolent and warlike. They were spending more time in our area, raiding camps and fish weirs. Our younger men were also becoming more warlike in their actions and, along with other radicals, were beginning to take vengeance on isolated Iroquois. In some cases they also fought against our more friendly neighbors, the Algonquin, who were very peaceful. Many times, on our trips, we came across a camp where the whole family had been wiped out and their possessions stolen. We would bury these people and try to identify them so we could notify the rest of the family or, in some cases, their tribe. Sometimes it was very difficult, because everything was stolen or that which was not had been torn up by animals. In one family we found the man and woman had been tortured and the young girls used by the warriors. They had not stolen a thing, but had done it just to amuse themselves. This made me very angry at the Iroquois and upset Fawn very much, but we both realized that the young men on both sides were guilty of this sort of thing. We would bury them and notify whomever we could. I had visited the Algonquin people many times in my travels and had made very good friends of a particular family. The man of this family and I had become blood brothers in a ceremony by their chief and Shaman. They had visited Fawn and me, and we had visited them in turn and we were indeed like family. His woman was a very gentle soul and a good mother. They had had four children and had lost six.

She knew much about growing a garden that his family had learned over many years, and she shared this knowledge with Fawn, who in turn taught her some of our ways. The man was not a good hunter but excellent in fishing, which was not a big thing as fish were most plentiful at certain times of the year. They just preferred fish to meat.

Our children had become good friends and had had many happy times together. He was an individual in his ideas, as I was, and did not always follow the customs of his people. There were many whom we considered our friends, and we visited them when we were near their camps. It was always difficult to lose such friends.

There were the people we had lived with that winter near the lakes and swamps, and the rice gatherers who were still guarding their little section of shoreline on the rice lake. We used to camp near them when we met Fawn's family there in the summertime.

The years seemed to go by very quickly now, and my family was beginning to grow up. I first noticed this when my son was not as quick to join me in a hunting trip but was hanging around the place where the women went to wash and swim. He would also be looking at his sisters, who were now developing, and was treating them with more respect. I was approached by many men in the tribe wishing to arrange a marriage between my son and one of their girls. In spite of our customs, I had no intentions of picking a mate for my boy and, though Fawn did not wholly agree, she went along with what I said. With our daughters she gave me to understand that she intended to strike the best bargain possible when their time came. I did not argue this point with her as she had made up her mind and would not listen to me in any case. She still had a mind of her own, and woe betide anyone that crossed her.

We met many of Fawn's people in our journeys and, though we were not bothered, we would have been had Fawn not spoken to them. If I had been alone in the forest I would have avoided them and would not have had trouble. But with the family along there was little chance of blending into the trees. We would sit by these people's fire pits at night and listen to their stories, and they were very interesting when they talked.

Most of them were family groups such as mine who had to go further and further from their own territory for game. They told us that the game had all but disappeared in their area. They showed no hostility to us, as long as we were friendly. It was the young ones that caused the trouble on both sides. They told us they had found many of their people who were killed and robbed by ours. This was regretted, but neither side could control our hot-blooded young. Those boys who were not involved soon learned this violence from the older ones. They would return with booty and tell stories of their bravery and the fun they had killing the enemy. If you condemned them you were looked down upon, and if you agreed with what they did you had your own conscience to contend with. As far as I was concerned, I did not give a damn if they looked down on me, for neither I nor mine would ever do these terrible things.

As time went on, Fawn and my family became more and more isolated from my village as things progressively got worse. My son finally picked his own mate about this time, and it was pleasing for me to find that his woman was the daughter of my old friend Winter Hawk, or Noisy Fingers as I still called him with great glee. We were still good friends despite the rivalry between us and we had many fond memories to share. When the ceremony to make them man and woman was over, my son went to the lodge of Winter Hawk to live for a year and to supply substance for his family, as is our custom. Besides this, I paid dearly to Winter Hawk for the woman, but she proved to be worth it, as she gave me a fine grandson of whom I was most proud.

About a year later my oldest daughter was spoken for by the son of my friends, the Algonquin family, and, though I was loathe to let her go, I found that Fawn and the mother of the boy had made these arrangements between them because the boy and my daughter were very much in love, and so I was pleased, as was his father. Apparently they had been attracted to each other for a long time and, though Fawn had noticed, I had not.

Kidnapped

About three months after this my youngest daughter was taken by the Iroquois in the forest while gathering berries. Three girls were captured, and another had hidden in the brambles and had spread the alarm. I was away hunting at the time and did not find out until I met a man on the trail to our village. I rushed home and Fawn was in a terrible state. She had packed the things I would need and I left that night. Finding the men who had tracked them for a distance before losing their signs, I got the location and traveled most of the night. The next day by noon I found where they had lost the trail. I looked for some sign to follow but could find none. I assumed they were aware they would be followed and had hidden all signs. I lay down and had a rest, then took the route I thought they would follow. That night I lay in a hollow between two logs and slept fitfully till before daylight. I had a quick meal of dried fish and took off in a southeast direction.

At noontime I climbed a ridge to look for campfires. I could see one in the far distance and headed in that direction. By late afternoon I came to the now-cold fire pit and looked for signs for trailing. I found their trail with no trouble and followed very carefully so as not to let them know I was behind them.

By darkness I could smell their campfire and slid and crawled until I could see the camp clearly. There were only two men, who appeared to be father and son. I crept up behind the eldest and, drawing my knife, jumped onto his back and held my knife to his throat. I warned the younger one to be still and asked them questions. They were Iroquois, hunting and on their way to the main camp where their families were. They had not seen any young men with Huron girls.

I released the old man and explained why I had done what I had. They showed much sympathy to me and made me welcome by the fire and fed me. I did not sleep by their fire, but went into the bush nearby and hid till morning, and then I accompanied them for the next day to their main camp. They questioned their families to find out what I was looking for but they could be of no help. I stayed with them that night, listening to their stories, and was surprised at the hardship some people were having because of the shortage of game in their areas.

The next morning I could do nothing else but head toward Iroquois land and hope to find word of them there. I traveled by night, and sometimes by day, to avoid running into any war parties, and lit no fires but ate raw meat and anything else I could find. I passed many fires in the night and I crept up to them to see if they were the ones I was after, but to no avail. After many days I arrived where I had to cross the water, and only because I was recognized by the old man with the canoe did I manage to get across without incident.

I was now coming near the area of Fawn's relatives and grew a little careless. I was attacked and bound by a war party before I knew what was happening. They examined my clothes and bags closely and knew I was a Huron, but the things I wore puzzled them because they showed I was associated with the Mohawk tribe. They kept me bound and questioned me. I explained why I was there and who I was. They listened and held a conference among themselves. They decided to take me to the camp I was looking for and to turn me over to Fawn's family, after a suitable financial arrangement could be struck. They fed me and tied me more comfortably, but because of the stories about me they kept close watch on me. The next morning, with a pole across my shoulders, my hands bound to it, and my feet tied loosely together so I could walk, we set off for the camp of the Mohawk.

When we arrived there I could recognize none of the people, but my captors showed no concern. They tied me to a pole in the center of the camp and left me there that night. The next morning they fed me and we went further to the south. We finally arrived at a camp just before dusk. I was tied to a tree a little distance away and my captors went into the camp, leaving two warriors with me. I was left there all that night, and early the next morning three of them came back with one of Fawn's relatives, whom I recognized but did not know well. They talked for a while and left again. The two left guarding me were eating and drinking but offered none to me and I was hungry and thirsty. About noon the other warriors came back and had a conference with the two guards, then they led me into camp.

When I saw Fawn's parents and other family members I was greatly relieved. They untied and fed me without a word and left me by myself for a while. Later they were to tell me they had to drive a hard bargain with my captors to get my release. I told them I would repay them for this. They questioned me closely about my daughter's kidnaping and about the time it happened. They asked about the other girls and what they were doing when captured. I had to describe them as best I could. I did not know the two girls well enough to give a good description. They sent runners the next morning to advise other camps that their granddaughter was missing and why. Other warriors took to trails in the area to hunt for the girls as well.

For the next two weeks or so I and others scoured the area nearby for leads to the girls' captors. Finally, a group of warriors remembered seeing a group from the neighboring tribe called the Oneidas with some prisoners, but they said there were more than three. The family decided that it would be more prudent if I stayed in camp while they went into this region, as the Oneidas were very unpredictable with Hurons. They were gone for more than twenty days and I was beside myself waiting for word. Finally, a runner came to camp with good news. They had found the girls and were negotiating for their release. At this point I would have paid anything for my girl's release and was also angry enough to attack their captors, but my relatives stayed my hand with reason.

Finally, a deal was made, and in a while I had my daughter back. She was unharmed, but very thin, and thankful I had come for her.

She clung to me for so long that our relatives had to pull her away so the women could tend her. It turned out that there were five other young children, two girls and three young boys, taken from our neighborhood. My friends returned again at my insistence to try to gain their release too. I told them I would repay them the cost in like goods. They returned sometime later and said they could get the other children, but a staggering amount was needed to come up with the full amount needed; they would try to get some arrangement made. Finally, it was agreed that they would accept one-third of the amount now and would expect the balance by the middle of next summer to be paid to Fawn's family by the rice gatherers' place. I gave my word on my honor, and the deal was consummated.

The five were given to us and they were overjoyed to see me, a Huron, in this country. The women of the tribe took care of the youngsters while I met with the men to work out what this had cost me. It came to a lot of furs, and other items like tools, weapons and stone. It was more than I had, but the parents of the other children would have to pay their share. This was a gamble, as some parents would not take back captured children for they believed the child was now possessed of demons or some stupid thing like that.

We now made plans to return to our own village, and, because of the way things were in regard to our safety, it was decided that we would be accompanied by a few men from Fawn's family as far as they could go.

We left in the morning and, after following many valleys

and climbing over ridges, we came to lakes that we were to follow that would lead us to the big river, which we had to cross by boat. This took many days, and we were always on our guard, even though we had the extra men with us.

The weather was now cooler in the evenings, and we had to keep moving if we were to make our own village before freeze-up. After we had crossed the wide river we were now into more friendly country. The trail led us along the north edge of the big lake, and we followed this for many days, meeting many more Iroquois, until we came to the river that led to the rice lake. The men from Fawn's village left us here and we were now on our own.

We spent most of the time looking for ways to avoid contact with other people. The two boys would go in front of us and let us know if anyone was ahead. This took valuable time that we could ill afford. When we were assured that the people we met meant us no harm, we would sit by their fires and explain what we were doing there. Most were very helpful, while other did not want to become involved with our problems.

During the days of traveling I was very concerned how my tribe would take to my committing them to pay a ransom for the girls and boys I had with me. There was no doubt they would help to pay it, but you must realize we were honor-bound by arrangements made by any member of the tribe in these cases. The whole tribe was committed by the actions by one member in all things, and the reputation of the tribe was never to be dishonored by any one member or he would be exiled forever.

I had never done anything before in this way. The children with me were well-behaved and did as I asked. I had met the girls before but had no knowledge of the boys. They were of our village but not my clan. They showed no fear now, as they had been through so much they had lost any fear they had. Our food was running low and it took some time to replenish it. When we came to the shallow lake where the rice people were, I looked for our old friends who, though not overjoyed to see us, treated us cordially. They gave us some food and some rice to take with us and we went on our way, as time was becoming critical if we were to make it home before freeze-up time. After we circled the end of the lake, I headed in a northwest direction, hoping to save time.

I had traveled some of this country before but had not come

in contact with the people there because I was unsure of them, and many of the Wyandot lived here as well. They were not the best of people. They were Hurons, but were the black sheep of the family, as you would say. They could not be trusted in anything and were bad people, stealing and killing only when they had their foes outnumbered, for they were also cowards. I knew them to be very dirty people, also.

We tried to hurry along, as it was now very cold, and snow could come at any time. Luckily it held off until we were on the east shore of the big lake to the south of our village; we now had to go around the top of it and over the narrow crossover between it and the lake to the north. Snow now covered the ground and made our walking very difficult. We were joined by others of our tribe, who heard us as we walked along without fear. They shared food and clothing with us as much as they could and helped us along until the village came into sight.

Home Again

People came running to meet us, and the joy of families reunited was very touching. As for myself, Fawn's scream of delight at seeing our daughter again was heartwarming, as well as her joy of seeing me alive too. People could not be contained in their welcome and tears of joy, and all were talking at once, prying me with questions. They sent for the families of the boys I had saved and they were soon reunited.

We were exhausted with our fast trip through the snow and our food problems and not having had enough clothing. We were soon filled with food and given dry clothing and a warm fire. We were soon asleep, even though people kept talking on and on and tried to question us further. I awoke early and the people were still about us. After a small meal I told them the whole story, from the time I left the village until our return, and the children filled in their part of the tale also. The whole tribe agreed that what I had done was the only thing to do, and they would pay the goods for the children's release. It would not be an individual thing—all the tribe would contribute. This took a load off my mind, as I had worried about this since making the deal with the captors. I would have had to work hard for two years to make up the things that were required to pay the ransom, if I had been required to pay it by myself.

You may wonder why we would pay, now that we had the children, but it was a matter of the tribe's honor, and the tribe's reputation was involved. Our commitment was now more important than the lives of the hostages had been. Their lives had affected but a few people, but all were now affected.

The tribal council took over the problem, and this freed me to start providing for my family again and to get back to my forest and hunting. The game was not as plentiful as it had been when I was younger, and there was more competition for it, since our tribes were getting larger. There was also the pressure of the Iroquois, who were now living closer and closer to our hunting grounds. The people closest to us were the Wyandot, who were not too popular, as I have stated. Not all the Wyandot were bad, but the majority were. The men were rather shiftless, though the women were, by necessity, hard working, and some were good hunters. Some of the women were very pretty and had a reputation for loose living with our men. The Wyandot changed chiefs quite often—usually by killing them. This was not a position much sought-after in their tribe. They would be quick to blame any bad luck on the hapless chief. One I heard of was called Chief Many Names. This, of course, was just a story told by our people to show the disdain in which we held the Wyandot. Chief Many Names was what we called a make-believe chief of theirs. What his real name was we did not know. It was said he was made a chief and, realizing what the fate of a chief usually was, he would change his name every month. He thus deceived the people into thinking they had a new chief and things would get better. It was said that he ruled the tribe for many years before the dolts caught on. At least, this is how the story went. I would sometimes meet these people in the forest, and I found them to be as reputed. We would not avoid them but tried to ignore them.

My family was growing, as my eldest daughter now had two children who were, as you know, part Huron and part Algonquin. They lived with us for over a year, and then left to live with their father's tribe. We would visit back and forth in the summers. Time flew past, or so it seemed.

We were now hearing more and more about the people with the white skin. One summer I went to the river with the high falls to our south on a trading trip to secure tobacco for our people.

The Niagras

Tobacco was used in many of our ceremonies, and some people smoked it all the time, like Pipe Eater had, though I did not, nor did any of my children. My mother had smoked, however, as had many of the other women. The people we traded with were very friendly and sincere. I had heard of a sacred waterfall and, being close, decided to see it. We could hear its voice from many miles away, and the thundering of it made us shake with fear.

When we broke from the forest beside the falls we were spellbound by the sight. I could only stand there, hypnotized by the water and the noise. Our friends told us that many people threw themselves into the swirling waters, so it was better not to stare at them for too long. We moved downstream a ways and looked back at it, and we were not so hypnotized as we had been nearer the falls. Our friends told us about the great spirit of the water, and how maidens were sacrificed to it at certain times to help improve their crops and their health. I found this a terrible thing, and my blood ran cold to think of a poor soul thrown into awful, violent water. Fawn and I left soon, as the cold chill of the water rose up among us.

I had heard of this waterfall before, but to be there and hear it was not good. While with these people, we were told of the white-skinned people that had been seen that summer, passing through their land with an Indian group guiding them. They had traded food and skins for many beads and a sheet of metal that showed your face when you looked into it. This I saw with my eyes. Looking into the metal I saw my own face, which did not please me much. It was ugly, with the many scars that I could now see more clearly than I had when looking into quiet water. My women made much of this and wished they had one also. I was sorry I had not seen these people with the white skin, as I was curious. I was also somewhat apprehensive because of the big stick they spoke about that made much noise and killed things. We quickly returned home and spent many hours by the fire pit, telling others of our trip to the great waterfall and about the people there.

Alone Again

That following spring my youngest daughter was spoken for, and my woman again made a good match on this one. She let me do the talking and bargaining, but she made the decisions and told me what to say. Everyone thought how smart I was to strike such a bargain, but it was Fawn, and not I, although I was not about to tell them although most of the women knew. Now, all my family had gone, and Fawn and I were alone, as we were when we started out. I was not too sad, but Fawn was very miserable for a while until the grandchildren started to come along. My youngest girl was nearby with her family, and my son now lived in the longhouse.

Fawn and I found ourselves going into the forest more than ever before, and we would usually stay away from the village for many months at a time. This is not to say we could neglect our garden, on which we had to rely more and more.

The family had grown so much that we had moved our garden further from the village, as had others, and when we were not there our family took care of it for us, as we always shared the bounty of our hunting and gathering with them.

We had to govern our actions by the seasons and the availability of food. In the spring we would get the new growth of vegetation and gather birds' eggs when we could. Some birds were so numerous at nesting time that we feasted on the eggs and the young for weeks. The birds were so thick in the air that, from a high vantage point, you could hit them with a stick and kill many. These birds, like the Huron, are no more, though they were then a good food source. The garden was now the most important part of our food supply, and much time was spent caring for it. Fawn, the girls, and their children worked at it more than the men did. I spent most of my time hunting, when possible. More and more I had to help with the gathering of nuts and berries. The woods were always filled with people, it seemed, and many of our favorite spots were now used by others.

Our village was the largest Huron one, but there were also other smaller villages not far from ours. Our population kept growing, and so did our needs for additional land for gardens and hunting. The same thing was also being experienced by other tribes. There was no real shortage of food; it just took longer and more effort to get it. In the warm weather there was no problem. It was the preparation and storage of the food for the cold winter months that kept us busy. It was always on our minds that you had to store this extra food to survive, and it drove us to our limit.

Close Call

When hunting parties intruded into our areas it made us angry, especially when they were Iroquois. I still liked to hunt alone, while most others preferred going with the hunting parties. This nearly cost me dearly many times. Once, in the fall season on a warm late afternoon, I was in a large, grassy clearing. In the middle was a large maple tree that had shed most of its colorful leaves about the ground. I lay down on the leaves and dozed off; then I smelled tobacco smoke and, looking around the tree, I saw a group if Iroquois break into the clearing. I thought of running but knew they would have me before I could go far. I gathered my bag and, keeping the tree between us, I crept to a gully which had been made by rain runoff near the large roots of the tree. I lay down in the gully, on my back, pushing leaves over me as deeply as I could, without making a hill of them. I breathed deeply to make it possible for me to take shallow breathes later.

I felt the Iroquois footsteps coming and knew when they were at the tree. I felt them drop their packs and fall to the ground. They talked for a while, then made camp. I could soon smell the strong smoke of their fire, and it seemed to lie in the hollow in which I was hiding. Soon the smell of their meal filled me with hunger, as I had not eaten since early morning and then only some cold meat. It must have been dusk when one of them came my way and stopped over me. Then I heard the sound of water hitting the leaves on my chest and realized that he was urinating on me. I could smell the stench as it ran over my chest and under my chin. I felt like gagging, but knew there would be worse fate if I were found. I seemed to hold my breath until he had left. I was thankful he had not done the other on me.

I lay there listening to them talk over their pipes until, one by one, they went to sleep. I could hear the slow steady breathing of one that must have been close to me. Soon they were grunting and turning in their sleep, and I slowly moved my arms and uncovered my face. The moon was shining and it was like daylight, so I knew I must be careful. There was a breeze once in a while that rustled the leaves, so I waited and moved only when the breeze made a noise to drown any sound I made.

I was soon on my stomach. It seemed that I crawled for hours before I could get to the grass and rise up on my knees, to move slowly away. Once, one of them awoke and, facing me, made water but, luckily for me, he was still sleepy and did not notice me. When I got to the woods I walked slowly and lightly away. About dawn I was far away, and when I came to a stream I jumped in and soaked away the urine and my nervous sweat and dirt. Even in the cold water it seemed I would never get the smell off.

Later that morning I came upon a friendly camp whose people were known to me, and they had a great laugh upon hearing my story, especially about being urinated on. They gave me much food to eat and, with a full stomach, I fell asleep by the fire sitting up. Later, the heat of the fire woke me as they prepared the evening meal, and I found the woman had covered my back with a skin to keep me warm while I slept. It had now turned quite cool, and it felt like frost in the air. I spent that evening and night with my friends and left the next morning. They were still laughing about my experience when I left.

I knew I must hurry home to help with the gathering of nuts for the winter. They were at their best after a frost, as were cranberries and some of the roots we gathered. The garden also had to be prepared for winter. Life went on as usual that winter, but the spring would be filled with events that would change and shorten the lives of most of us in my village.

Getting Older

I was now somewhere in my fortieth summer. This made me an elder of the village, though I refused to think that way. Most of the men who had grown up with me had gone long ago, as I was old among my people, though not the oldest. Most were dead by their thirty-fifth summer. My face was like leather, so my scars blended in more now. I was still tall and thin of stature and in fairly good shape. Fawn still showed the beauty she had when young, but had added a few inches to her width. This was common in our women after having children. She was still very active and would sometimes put me to shame with her boundless energy. She never complained and always had a cheery smile for me. She was now more concerned with my well-being than ever before and hated it when I went into the forest alone. After hearing my story of the clearing and my close call, she was ever more worried. That winter she would not leave my side.

Once I went with a group who knew where a bear had holed up to sleep for the winter, to get it for meat. She insisted on coming along and, after the others had disposed of the bear, it was discovered that it was a female with two new babies. Nothing would do but that Fawn brought them home, and the winter was taken up with the care and feeding of two ugly-tempered little black bears.

All the tribe had a hand in their care, but it was Fawn who was their adopted mother. Soon everything in our camp had teethmarks in it, even our hides. I was continually chasing them away from my bedding. In the spring they were thrown outside to stay, and they followed whoever paid them any attention. After being around camp for about two summers they had to be dragged away into the forest so they could leave us alone. They were now dangerous and ugly brutes who could do a lot of harm. But they were always gentle with Fawn and the other women and children. They used to fight with the dogs and had killed some before we got rid of them.

I only mention these bears because it was while hunting for some small fresh game to feed them that I saw my first white-skinned man. I was close by a small waterfall, on top of a rock cliff, looking down the river when canoes came in sight. By their number I thought it might be a war party. When they reached the falls I knew they would have to carry the canoes to the river above, so I decided to hide by the trail to see who they were. Even from this distance I could see some colors unfamiliar to me. I went back a ways near the trail, where I knew they must pass and where I could be well hidden. Little did I know the surprise in store for me.

10. White Man

I pressed my face into the soft moist moss as I heard them approach, holding my breath until it felt like my lungs would explode. At last their footsteps receded along the trail and I lifted my head to listen as they went on. I had first heard them coming as their feet made loud noises as they passed over the granite of an outcrop a good distance away.

At first I thought my mind was playing tricks on me when they came in sight a half-mile away. They had white skin and were wearing clothes of a kind and color I had never seen or imagined. On their feet were hard shoes, not moccasins. They carried long sticks in their hands and wore hats of a colored cloth. The Indians with them were not strangers to me, but were Wyandot. Many times they had traded with my people and had been friendly to us. They were known as "the people by the big river."

I suddenly realized that I could be seen by them, and dropped into a clump of sweet fern near the trail. Even with the fragrance of the sweet fern I could smell a bad odor coming from the white people, who did not smell at all like Indians. There were five of the white people and about thirty Indians in the group. They were sweating and grunting with the labor of walking the steep part of the trail and spoke in angry tones, as the black flies were at their worst at this time of year. This was the beginning of the fifth moon of your year (May).

The Indians and the white people carried many bundles and canoes, so I knew they had come a long way by water and were portaging to the lake above. It suddenly dawned on me that they were going to my village and panic struck me for my people. I had to wait until they were out of sight before I could start running as quickly as I could through the forest, taking every short cut I knew. As I ran, I was filled with apprehension and wondered what they wanted from us. I finally broke through the forest, near my home, and told Fawn what I had seen while I tried to get the chiefs and council together to tell them.

I had no sooner finished telling my story when the first canoe came in sight around the point. The chiefs went into council and stayed out of sight while many young braves gathered their weapons and stood on the shore to await their coming. I went with Fawn to a hill above the bay to observe what went on. All the canoes were now in sight, and it seemed to take forever for them to make shore. They stood away a bit while the Indians in the canoes talked to our men on shore. They then approached and landed.

The men on shore stepped back to give the strangers room to land. The women and children stood well back as they were not sure of these people. After they had landed they stood there as though waiting for something. Then our line of men opened to let the men from our council through to speak with them. Our chiefs did not come from the council house.

I will try to explain how these men impressed me. First of all the smell from these men was terrible. The two I took to be leaders wore round hats with wide brims of a dull brown color. Under the hat they wore a colored cloth tied at the back of the head. They had loose-fitting brown shirts with long puffy sleeves. Their pants were tight and ended just below the knee. They had tall loose-fitting boots with a heel higher than the toe. One man had on a rough-looking robe from his shoulders to above his feet. It was tied at the waist with the same cloth. He wore a chain around his neck with a cross on it and carried a square thing in one hand and a cross in the other. On his feet were flat, open shoes.

The rest of the white people wore cloths around their heads, with straggly hair showing, and had on loose, rough shirts that were pulled on over their heads. They had pants that were rough and ended hanging above their knees. Their shoes were short, with the heel again being higher than the toe. They were very dirty and sweated a lot. Most were roughly bearded. The leaders were also bearded, but their beards appeared to be trimmed occasionally.

After the men had landed, the white men began to unload the canoes and many cloth bundles, round wooden kegs, and long wooden chests were deposited on shore. The man in the long robe knelt on one knee and talked, then waved the little iron cross about. He was later to be poking this thing into the face of everyone he met. One man went to a chest and removed a piece of very colorful cloth and gave it to the head of our council. One Wyandot came forward and told our people what the white man said. They talked for a while, through the Wyandot, and our council left to go to the chiefs in the council house. The white men stood about, smiling and talking to the people. They talked in a musical voice, and it seemed one word was linked to another. Our language was made of short words or you could sometimes use grunts. After a moment a man came from the council house. He talked to the Wyandot and explained that the white people were welcome and said the chiefs would see them later. They were shown a small lodge near the water where they were to stay. The Wyandot, except for one interpreter, were to remove themselves down the shoreline, away from the village.

After inspecting the lodge, one man told the others to bring in the chests and bundles. After this the men who were dressed in the poorer clothes removed them and, with great joy, jumped into the water to clean themselves.

The people on the shore laughed at them and some joined them in the water. Fawn and I laughed as we sat on the hill and watched as the men ran about, their white skin flashing in the sun. The women were looking at the men and now began making lewd remarks and showing interest in their sexual parts. The men were not different, just white. The men took knives and shaved themselves, looking into the metal that reflects. The other two men came from the lodge and joined the others and washed and shaved off some hair. They then dressed in cleaner clothes.

The women of the tribe now gave them food, and some of the white men tried to talk to the women, who knew not what they said, but just giggled and flirted with them. You must remember, these white people had come a long way, mostly by canoe, and were very dirty and tired. The Wyandot were usually a dirty, lazy lot anyway. The interpreter now began to bargain on behalf of the white men for women to cook and wash for them and other things. We were to find these men had a sexual appetite that could not be satisfied; we wondered what their women were like. Fawn and I maintained our distance from them for a few days. Many of the young women in the tribe began to wear beads and colored clothes and feathers, mirrors and combs, and we all knew how they got them. Many times I saw them in the water playing together, not only the men, but also their leaders—even the one they called a priest or Shaman.

Our son, who lived in the longhouse with his wife and family, was in close contact with these people and knew what was going on as far as their wants went.

The day after they arrived, the chiefs let it be known they would greet the newcomers. I went and stood nearby so I could observe what went on. First the leader and his sub-leader came out from their lodge, and what a sight they made. The leader was the most impressive. On his head was a large brimmed hat of gold color with a purple feather, from what kind of a bird I could not imagine. His face was a startling white, like it had not been before, and he now had long white curled hair that he had not had before. I was later to learn that he could take this hair off at will, and that he put this white powder on his face to appear more white than he was. He wore a coat that was the same color as his hat, and it had shiny metal buttons and braid. His vest, under this, was a purple color, and under this was a shirt with many frills on the neck and wrists. He also carried a small white piece of cloth with frilled edges that he kept putting to his nose for some reason.

His pants were tight and an off-colored white. They ended below his knees with a bright-colored gold band. His legs, from his knees to his boots, were covered in white stockings. His shoes were white and had a high heel, and they buttoned in the front and went up to his ankle. On his hip was a belt from which hung a long, pointed metal blade. The other one was dressed in a like manner, but not as elaborately, and instead of metal sword he had a long gun. The priest had on the same clothes as he came in, only cleaner. He still had the large metal cross, which he kept waving at people, and kept saying things in a language that was different from the others.

Our chiefs were seated on furs, and they did make a handsome scene with their colorful feathers and clothes. They deemed this such an important occasion that they went all out to impress these strangers. They made much ceremony, and soon the strangers were seated also. The Wyandot interpreter was kept very busy for the next few hours. Soon the strangers' servants brought out a chest from their lodge and the leader gave our chiefs many gifts, including a very hard, sharp knife, of which I was envious. Our chiefs gave them a skin with much decoration on it and many tools of flint, such as knives, scrapers, arrows and a bow. They all sat and talked for some time, then retired to their own lodge.

I walked back slowly and came across one of their men using a metal tool like a tomahawk to cut points on small saplings that they were using in their camp. I watched with curiosity, and the man handed me the tool so I could examine it more closely. It was the first time I had touched metal, and it felt cold and hard to my hand. It was wrapped around a piece of hard wood that served as a handle. The man smiled and handed me a piece of wood and indicated that I should strike it with the tool, which I did. It went through the branch with such ease that I was surprised, and the man laughed. What a weapon that would make.

I had a similar tool called a tomahawk, but it did not match this. It had a stone head, which was a new idea for our people. Before this we had only a stick with the knot of a tree at the end to serve as a club, which I had used for many years. The white men then took from his waist a metal knife, which he handed to me, and indicated I should cut the wood with it, which I did. It did a good job and cut through the wood very quickly.

I took out my flint knife and handed it to him and he tried it. Mine was sharper but would break easily whereas his could be resharpened and mine could not. The fact that the metal knife wouldn't break was my reason for wanting one. I also liked the length of the blade. We smiled at one another and I went on my way. By the way, he was about as ugly as I.

When I returned to my lodge I had to explain in detail everything I had seen to Fawn, who was with my daughter-in-law and my grandson. My son was active in the council for our clan, as was my brother, but I stayed clear of any of the meetings. My daughter-in-law told us that the white men were telling the chiefs that they wanted our help to fight the Iroquois, and had approached neighboring tribes also. It appeared that a large meeting of the entire tribe was to take place in a few days in our village, and a decision would then be made about what they wanted and expected of us. This was very disturbing news to Fawn and me, as they were, in effect, asking us to fight our own family on her side. I decided to attend the meeting and to make my views known within our tribal council.

The Beginning of the End

This was a most miserable time in my life, and it is difficult to describe why, because the events happened swiftly and I seemed powerless to do anything. The white people were very smart in their approach, and very persuasive, and made many promises to us. The weapons they had and the great number of people they seemed to organize among us made us think we had a good chance to drive the enemy from our land for all time. Most of the people were delighted to have the chance to make this happen, and it seemed to them that this was a good way to bring it about.

I knew that it would be difficult to argue against them, because the others were very much taken with the white people and felt that their arms would make the difference against the Iroquois, who were very fierce fighters while we were not. I spent the next two days talking to any of my people with influence I could find and made my views known. I did not get much sympathy from them, though they did listen politely.

When our neighbors from surrounding areas had gathered there was a meeting to listen to the white man's proposals and, though they argued for more than a week about it, they finally agreed to join the white man and fight. The next few weeks were spent arranging and getting the expedition supplied. I spent a lot of time observing the white man's camp, and one day a boy took a small piece of colored cloth from a stick where it had been laid to dry. The white men seized him and made such a fuss that some of our men came running. The white men wanted the boy punished, but we could not understand this. Among our people there is no such thing as stealing. Everything belongs to all and is shared. We knew that things were not for the taking, and things necessary for one's survival were to be left alone. We knew the white man did not understand our ways and also that they did not want to make trouble with us. There were other instances that occurred that were disturbing to me, but it was obvious that these things would make no difference to my people, who continued to prepare for the expedition with good spirit. I was chosen, along with others of my age, to stay at the village and guard the women.

I found this insulting but held my tongue. I had no wish to fight the other members of my own family. My son went with the war party, but my brother, like myself, was considered too old. The morning the war party left to meet with others at the narrows between the two lakes I also left, taking the trail south beside the big swamp, and I hurried to the lake below. It took me many days, and I traveled both night and day, resting only when I had to. When I finally arrived by the lake I met many Iroquois, who agreed to hurry home and give messages to Fawn's family about what was happening. They were not really surprised at what was going on, as they knew about the white man and what they were doing. They assured me they were prepared and would not give up because of the white man's weapons.

I then hurried as fast as possible homeward. Just before entering camp I killed some game and carried it into the village to show I had just returned from a hunt. A few days after I went again into the forest and saw where the tribes had gathered before going south. I found many women setting up camp there to await the return of their menfolk. This would be a long wait, and for many their menfolk would never return. I went into the forest and returned the next day with a fat deer for them and spent a few days helping those I could. I went with them to the river and helped to gather fish and also to set up drying racks with the help of some of the older children.

I then returned to my village, and it seemed I spent most of the summer bringing in game and doing other chores that were sometimes strange to me.

Fawn did as much as she could, along with the younger women and old people. You can imagine the amount of work now necessary, because we had to feed all the people there and also to lay in food for the coming winter. Everyone worked hard and shared the work. Food seemed to be in better supply, perhaps because the forest was without our hunters and the usual influx of Iroquois.

I Find a Child

On one trip to the south of our village, I was about two days away when I came upon a camp of Iroquois from the area to the southeast, by the big lake. They had recently been raided, by whom I had no idea. The man and woman had been killed, as well as one child of about six years. The camp had been vandalized and things of use taken. It looked like a hurried raid because much was left untouched. It must have happened within the past ten hours. I buried the people and went through the camp, trying to find something to identify them. I suddenly tensed, because I heard a small sound. I lay on the ground straining to hear. I smelled the air again to catch anything strange. Again I heard a small sound and searched about. I went into the lean-to, or lodge of branches, and pulled away some of the furs and brush used to sleep on. Near the back was a bundle that moved and made a small sound. I pulled my knife and raised the furs, and there was small baby. I could scarcely believe my eyes. I picked it up and took it out into the sunlight. It was very weak and, I must say, very dirty. I cleaned it as best I could and wrapped it in furs. It made many weak sounds and I felt so helpless. I knew it must be fed soon or it would die, so I took out some of my dried meat and put it in water, that I brought to a boil.

After the water had cooled, I tried to feed the child, but it was hard. I again wrapped it and, tying it to my back, took off through the forest, looking for a woman with milk. I went to many camps but there were only men. That evening, after dark, I saw a campfire, and luckily there was woman with milk who agreed to feed the baby. When the child was put to her breast the woman cried out in pain, for the child was so starved it nearly tore her breast off. After a while the woman smiled and everything went well. She cleaned the baby and did all that was usual, and the baby slept. The next day I was preparing to leave when they told me to take the baby with me. I was surprised, because I thought they would keep the child, but they said they had no intention of keeping the child because it was girl and they had enough of their own. I had not thought of the sex of the child, as I did not think it mattered, but it apparently did to some. There was no use in arguing with the people, so I bundled the child up and took off through the bush again toward my village.

That evening I was close to a village of my own people, although it was not my village. I entered through the palisade and went to the lodge of the bear tribe. After looking for a while, I found a woman who would feed the child and clean it again, as it was beginning to smell bad. The next morning I left this village and, by night, was back to my own. Fawn was most motherly toward the baby and sent herself to find a woman to feed it while I explained what had happened to the people around me. They spread out through the village trying to find someone who would know the family, but did not find anyone, so we finally realized the family must have been Iroquois and it was our people who had killed them all except for the baby. Most of the warriors were away with the white men, so it must have been an older group of hunters. The baby was now the responsibility of our tribe, and it was up to us to find a family who could care for it. As the final decision was left to me, I picked, out of all suggested, a young woman Fawn told me about who had lost a baby a few days before. The woman was happy beyond belief, and we knew she would raise her as her own.

The War Ends For Us

News was now coming back to us about the expedition to the south. Some men who had hurt themselves by accident on the way had returned to tell us that they had met the odd group of Iroquois and had dispatched them with no trouble. They were going slowly because of the necessity to find food on the way. They had lived mainly off the land as they went. Some of the more exuberant warriors had tried to push on ahead but were being restrained by the white leader. One man brought us word from our son, who said that he was in good health.

In the next few days more and more men would be returning from the wars, and many would tell us of those killed. There was much wailing in many lodges during the coming months as bad news was received about loved ones. I and the other men of the village did what we could to keep the people supplied with food. We fished and dried the catch and gathered nuts and berries with the women for the winter months.

Near the time of the first snowfalls the men began returning and told us they had been beaten badly by the Iroquois, who even pursued them back to our village. The white leader had been wounded and was with some of our men. They said he objected to being brought to our village but was really too ill to escape from us. He was carried on a travois and put into the Shaman's lodge where he could be cared for. His friends were put into the same lodge they had occupied before leaving. We did not at the time put any blame on these people for our defeat but realized we were just no match for the Iroquois. We still felt more secure having them and their weapons with us.

During the next few months the white leader's strength returned, and by spring he was taken over land and by canoe to much of our surrounding area. He showed much interest in our territory and wanted to see and meet all the people he could. By midsummer we felt more secure because the Iroquois had not come seeking revenge, so the white people prepared to leave us. The day before they were to leave, the white leader and two of his men came up the hill to my lodge, where I was sitting by my fire pit with Fawn and my grandsons. He stopped to talk with us and asked why I did not live in the longhouse. I told him. He said he had been told that I had many fine furs and wanted to trade for some. Fawn brought out the furs she had bundled and stored and also some she had made into moccasins and bags. They admired her work, which pleased her.

They put aside some of the finer pieces and offered to trade for them. They offered Fawn a comb, the polished metal to look at your face, and some beads of many colors, but generally white. They offered me the same, but I refused, requesting instead a metal knife and an axe. After much bargaining they agreed, much to my surprise. They took most of the finest pelts and much of Fawn's needle work. We were happy about the trade and many said we had made a fine bargain.

The white man sat and talked through the interpreter for some time, asking me many questions. They asked me if I would like to accompany them to their village by the big river, where I could learn more of their ways, which I declined to do. The next day they left, and many of our people left with them. We did not realize how many until later, when more slipped from our village to follow them. These people we were never to see again.

The white man in the robe with the cross around his neck did not leave with the others, but stayed about a month, later taking with him some who believed his medicine. All told there must have been about a thousand people who left the territory at this time. They were from many other villages also, but mainly from ours. Our clan was not affected as much as others were. Our chiefs and council discouraged the people from leaving and would not go themselves. Some did leave with others, though. Among them was my youngest daughter, who went with her man and took our grandchildren with them. This made us very sad, and Fawn was beside herself with grief for quite a while. We did not know at the time that we would not see them again.

We were now kept very busy with the harvest for the winter. There was much sadness in the village because of the people leaving and because of the men missing from the war. Many nights were spent in ceremonies for the dead and the missing, as all were to have a ceremony for their departure. My old friend Noisy Fingers was not among those that went away. But he had died from an accident since, and this grieved me much. My metal knife and axe were put to good use in the winter, cutting wood for the fire pit. Many people borrowed the axe and were most careful with it, keeping it sharp and changing the handle when necessary. The knife I kept for myself, as it would not hold an edge like my flint one did but was always needing sharpening on sandstone. Fawn would not use it to skin animals, as she preferred her own.

11. My Last Days

I Lose My Son

Spring seemed to take a long time coming this year, and we were most happy when it did finally come, allowing us to leave the camp for the woods more often. It was during this spring that I lost my son to the Iroquois, who were now beginning to show up in war parties in the area and would attack those in small groups. My son had been out with a hunting party when they were surprised by a larger group of Iroquois. This indeed made my heart heavy and, though we tried to track down the Iroquois, we did not succeed in finding them. My daughter-in-law was now left to the care of her older brother, and my grandson was left for us to care for. This made the pain a little more bearable. The youngster was now five years of age, and the families thought it best if I were to teach him the things necessary for his survival.

After all the suitable ceremonies were done for my son and the other killed, we quickly returned to our problems of hunting, gardening, and gathering from the forest. We now had to travel in larger groups, and it took all the skill one possessed to stay clear of war parties. Neither Fawn nor I had any word from her family, and we were concerned about their safety in the past conflict. My eldest daughter, who had moved to the Algonquin tribe with her man, could no longer make the trip to see us in safety, so Fawn and I made the trip alone to visit her. We traveled by dark, avoiding any campfires and sleeping in caves or dense brush during the day. We made no fires and ate dried food. When we made it to the Algonquin camps, our daughter and family were most joyous to see us. We had to recount the story of her brother's death, and this made us all sad.

Before long we were visiting and telling our stories around many campfires. The Algonquins were expecting the same problems with the Iroquois that we were. There had been raids into their villages by war parties, and they had lost many people. Some of the group had left to go to the village of the white people, while most had gone north to the villages of the Ojibwas, who were their relatives. After a month with them we made our way homeward again, traveling with the same caution we had before.

On our arrival at our village, we found many people had left, traveling southwest with the Wyandot people who were gradually headed that way. Many of the men who had been injured during the expedition to the Iroquois land were dying from their wounds, and we had ceremonies every night for them, or for those who were leaving in order to get good spirits for our time.

Things seemed to get progressively worse, and many times we sent delegates to the Iroquois to make peace; but they were too involved with their own problems to agree to anything. Though we did have a few peaceful intervals, we could not let our guard down because we never knew when we could be attacked. This went on for a long time.

I do not want to give the impression that we didn't do our share of fighting and sending out war parties. We were always searching for the enemy, and much killing and torturing took place. With the death of my son and Noisy Fingers and my other friends, I became more and more depressed. Also, the departure of my daughter and her family filled me with sorrow. I suddenly began feeling older and more useless, and if my grandson had not been with me I would have gone on the warpath myself to end it all. The fact of the matter was that I was getting old, and it showed in my actions. Hunting and fishing were now boring and did not arouse my interest as they once had. I became more content to sit by my fire pit and talk.

A lot of time was now spent strengthening the palisade that circled the main village. My lodge was now just outside the wall. Years before I had been some distance away from it, but population increases had expanded the village. My axe from the white man was in use constantly, cutting down and pointing small saplings to make poles for the wall. During this time my grandson and I would go to the forest and stream for food as often as possible, or as necessity demanded, but my spirit was not in it. I was healthy enough, except that my old wounds would cause me to be stiff and sore when it was cold and damp.

I Lose Fawn

It was during one of these trips that the end of my existence began. My grandson and I were by the river, near the place where it flowed into the big lake to the north of us. We had taken some fish from our weirs when we heard many voices and feet coming toward us from the west. We immediately went into the water and hid in the bulrushes. We lay there for over an hour until the owners of the voices came into view near some reeds that allowed us to see them. They were Iroquois warriors, and they numbered close to three hundred or so. I was afraid they were going to make camp on the shore beside us, but they continued on along, just past us around the bend in the river. I could see the smoke from their fire pits.

We stayed where we were, listening to them talking and, from what I heard, knew they were only half of the party. These had come to attack our village from the southwest. They also talked about the last village they had destroyed, not far from us. Soon their squaws and older people came into view, carrying the spoils of war from their last raid along with their camp supplies.

When they had settled down, my grandson and I made our way slowly along the shore until we were far enough away to avoid them, then came ashore. We headed south until we came to a camp of our people. I explained to them what we knew, and they agreed to go east to a small village of ours and take my grandson with them while I brought news to our village of the planned attack. We ate the fish we had brought raw so as not to make fire, and I hurried on my way to my village.

I arrived just at daybreak and saw smoke in the air before I got there. When I arrived, the scene before me was terrible. Part of the palisade had been torn down and some buildings were still burning. Bodies of my people lay everywhere, and screams of pain and anguish filled the air. I rushed down the hill to my own lodge and there, in front of it, lay my Fawn. She was covered with blood, and when I picked her up to take her inside the lodge I knew she was dead. I moaned and gave a great cry of anguish as I carried her into the lodge and laid her upon her furs. I sat there stunned, looking at her in disbelief that her own kind had killed her. About an hour later I went outside and looked around, and then it struck me. She had been killed by my own people.

I grabbed my axe and rushed toward the village, but before I could do any damage I was seized by some men of the village and held tightly. They explained that the women of the tribe, because of their own losses of loved ones, had turned on Fawn for revenge, because she was kin of the Mohawk. My mind was numb with anger and pain at what they had done. They left me lying on the ground where I lay until midday and then, not knowing what I was doing, I went into the forest, bumping into trees and walking through swamps, not seeing or caring.

I wandered like this for three days and found myself not far from the village where my grandson had been taken. I went into the village and, seeing my grandson rush over, I picked him from the ground and hugged him so hard he cried out. The people gathered about and someone told me they had thought I had been lost with the others of the village which had been overrun by the Iroquois.

My Village Destroyed

I suddenly remembered I had gone to my village to warn them but had not. The bitterness within me made me not care now. Somehow they knew about Fawn and how she had died, and many showed me great pity but could understand the feelings of the women of the tribe. I stayed with them that night and knew they were going to abandon their village and go toward the land of the Ojibwas, who were not our friends but still not our enemies. My grandson and I left the next morning to go back to our village. We passed many people on our way, some going to other more safe areas, others trying to find loved ones. There were many of our men looking for small bands of enemy tribes to fight for revenge. We also came across many camps with dead people who had been caught and killed by the Iroquois. These we buried as best we could. We were continually on guard and took much care to avoid people until we were sure of who they were. It was a miracle that I had not run into any people while I was wandering about during the few days after I had left the village. It took us nearly five days' journey to our destination and we were not happy when we got there.

The place was indeed a shambles. Hardly a longhouse stood without some damage. The palisades had been burned and pulled down in places. On the hilltop the ground was like a worked field, with so many new graves. I was told later that over two thousand of our people had been killed. Whole families had been wiped out, and so many still died from wounds each day that they could not keep up with the chore of the ceremonies and burials.

I went to my own lodge which, surprisingly, was still standing. I entered to find another family taking refuge there. I bid them stay with me and looked for Fawn's remains which, in my grief, I had not buried. They told me that the Iroquois had buried her, as was their custom, and showed me her grave. For the next two days I sat by her grave, while they took my grandson with them to my lodge. The women carried food to me, but I never ate.

On the third day I went into what was left of the village and looked for the Shaman. He was in his lodge, exhausted by so many ceremonies. I asked him to do the usual ceremony for Fawn, which he refused to do. In my anger I pulled my knife and, grabbing him by the throat, threw him out on the ground. He showed much fear and ran ahead of me to Fawn's grave where he began the proper ceremony without pause. After he was finished I felt rather sorry for what I had done, but I was still too bitter with my people to care much.

I returned to my lodge and gathered all I wanted to take with me and left much beside the graves of Fawn, my son, and Pipe Eater and his family. I then asked the people to leave, and then burned my lodge to the ground. After this I took my grandson and went into the forest, the only place where I could find any contentment. As I reached the top of the hill by the graveyard, I turned and looked down at what was left of the village and at my own lodge, still smoldering. Though there were still about three thousand people left there,

I felt completely alone for the first time in a long time. I thought of the people I had known and what they meant to me, and I felt a hard lump in my throat as I turned and hurried away.

Leaving My Land

I went around the large lake to the north, toward the land of the Ojibwas, but did not plan to go to them. I had known of a river there with a waterfall that would be a good place for me to stay awhile and wait for things to return to normal. I knew that I would never return to my village or my people. It was my intention to later try to make my way to the land of the Mohawk and join up with Fawn's family so my grandson could be raised with his own. After traveling for seven days, we finally found the waterfall and I spent some time building a small lodge.

I continually worked myself to exhaustion so I could sleep at night, to escape the thoughts that came into my head. Even then I would lie awake nearly all the time. My grandson showed his concern for me, as I was now not much more than a walking skeleton. I had cut my hair myself, so it was very uneven, and it was gray. My grandson would look at me and smile to himself, not wanting to offend me. The winter came and went and, in early spring, while we were below the falls fishing, a group of Ojibwas came to my lodge. They stood on the bank top, looking down on us without speaking. Bidding my grandson to keep on fishing, I went up the hill to where they stood and greeted them in a friendly manner. They stood silent for a moment; then, realizing that there was no harm in an old man and a young boy, they became friendly. They asked many questions then placed their camp near mine and shared my fire pit.

There were twelve of them: two men, six women, and four children. They were shorter than we were and more portly. They wore rougher-skinned clothes than we did, but they had many things that showed greater care and skill than ours. They could make handsome moccasins, and their decorations on skins were better than ours though the skins were not as well tanned. Their bead work was also well done. The women were rather coarser-featured than ours, but had well-developed figures. We had long talks that night over the fire pit and became good friends. I had a woman in my bed that night the first time in a long while.

The next day we spent loafing about and talking and eating as old friends. They knew of our troubles with the Iroquois, since many of our people were coming into their area to stay alive. They had been welcomed for the most part, but not in some areas. The Ojibwas told me that I could stay here as long as I wanted, but not to go further north. They would leave the one woman with me to save us from their people. I knew this was not so, but rather that they were glad to get rid of her. She was a relative they had inherited who was a nuisance to them, as they had to provide for her. I did not really mind, because it gave us someone to do the cooking and other womanly chores of a family. The Ojibwas stayed for a month or so, then unexpectedly vanished, taking with them their camp and a goodly part of mine also.

As this was a pretty place, we decided we would stay. In the meantime I made a bigger lodge, and the storage area was soon filled with food and furs.

My grandson was becoming a good hunter and provider, and the woman was a good worker and did much to make our life easy. She never complained, and she kept a good lodge. We both became very fond of her. It had not, however, left our minds that I would someday take my grandson to the Mohawk. Due to the good food and care of the woman I was soon back to my usual weight, and I felt much stronger. The woman cut my hair now, and it looked much better too. I would still wake in the night and feel so alone without my village and Fawn that I would get up and wander into the forest. Sometimes I would wander for days, then return hungry and exhausted again. The woman said the bad spirits were getting control of me, at which I laughed. Many happy evenings were spent about the fire pit with my grandson, telling him about the days past and about our people and how they had lived in days gone by. He was always interested in stories about Pipe Eater and Noisy Fingers. He had a ready laugh and, like me, had a love for the forest and its animals. When he was about twelve I decided that we would try and get to Mohawk country. We knew that the risk was now even greater than before, because of the fighting going on between us, and that our warriors were getting the worst of the battles.

Our people were leaving the area at a greater pace than ever. It was almost a panic situation. This we learned from travelers near our camp. I decided to travel over the trail to the northeast for a while, thus avoiding the area where the fighting was at its worst.

The Ojibwas woman stayed at the camp and we left almost everything with her, taking only what was necessary for our survival. She was sorry to see us go but did not try to stop us. I knew that, with what we had left her in food and furs and other goods, she would not be long in getting another man to move in—probably one of her own tribe. I knew I would never return, though I did not mention this to my grandson. I also knew my time was getting near, as age was now upon me. My eyes would cloud, my hearing was no longer acute, and I missed many of the smells on the wind.

We left early in the morning, while the mist was still in the air. The day was warm and no clouds hid the sky. We traveled many days without seeing anyone. I spent most of the evenings telling my grandson about the Mohawks and Fawn's family. He found it hard to understand how they could be our enemies here and still be related to him. We both still wore the small leather thongs about our necks that showed we were both Huron and Mohawk, if one understood how to read them. Fawn had made them for us years before. Outside of dried fish and berries, we carried no food. I was now getting very desolate in my body, and I knew my time was very near. I would sometimes smell the past and my old friends in the still air and knew they beckoned me. I was now driven to complete my quest for some Mohawk who would take my grandson to their camp. It was soon to happen in a very unexpected way.

The Last Chapter

We were now quite far south, near the area of many swamps and lakes, close to the lake of much rice, when the trouble started. We were skirting a rather large swamp, with my grandson ahead of me, when I felt a blow to my back and I knew I had been hit with an arrow. I fell forward, pulling my grandson under me to protect him as I fell to the ground. I felt a hand grab my hair and pull back my head, and then I heard a shout.

I looked up to see a warrior with a raised tomahawk ready to crash into my skull. A hand reached out and held his and I heard a man say, "Do not hit him, it is Red Snake." They raised me from the ground and took my grandson from under me. "This boy is also his." They tore the thongs from our necks and looked at them for a while, then lowered me gently to the knees. My grandson put his arms around my shoulders and hugged me. The blood was coming into my throat now and I could feel the pain of more than one arrow in my back. I had only felt the one hit but knew there were more.

The one who led the party asked why I was there, and I could not answer for choking on blood. My grandson answered them, saying I was taking him to his family in the Mohawk country because all our family here were dead. They told him they were Mohawk and knew of me and had seen me years before in their country with Fawn's family. They now leaned over me and, wiping away the blood from my face, tried to get me to understand them. I nodded my head in answer. They were sorry to have done what they did but had not recognized me in time. They said they would now be duty-bound to see that my grandson was taken to his Mohawk family, and on this they gave their word.

They asked what they could do for me and I indicated that they should place me over a low hanging branch, facing the swamp, and leave me to go in peace. They gathered my things together and, picking me up very carefully so as not to disturb the arrows which they could not remove, they carried me to the edge of the swamp and put me in a sitting position, draped over a limb of a fallen tree. My grandson came around to face me, and I explained that I must now go to my ancestors' home in the sky to be with his parents and his grandmother. He clung to me, sobbing until I pushed him away, and then they left. I watched them recede from the corner of my eye. I knew my grandson would be well taken care of.

I knew my time was near as the pain became more unbearable. Blood still came from my mouth, choking me and making it hard to breath. I looked over the swamp and I thought back to Fawn and our happy life together and about our children. Toward the white man I felt no ill will, as they had only made things happen a little sooner than they normally would have.

I looked out over the swamp at the water, calm in the summer evening. The surface was rippled now by a beaver as he swam about his business, and there was the occasional flop of a frog jumping into the water from his lily pad. I could see the leafless dead trees stand out lined against the low hills behind. The evening sky was now turning red as the sun began to ebb behind the trees.

My breathing became more labored and the pain began to dull. The evening was now filled with the sound of a bullfrog chorus setting up a great din. Suddenly, all was quiet as a deer came to the shore to drink. I heard a porcupine chewing on a branch nearby, and the splash of some animal entering the water.

My hearing must have improved near the end, because these were sounds I had not heard for some time. The frogs started up their songs again and soon filled the air, drowning out any other sounds. I could barely see now, and the sounds became further away as I descended into the dusk. Now I could hear no sounds and I became more calm and peaceful as I slipped into darkness. As the sun finally went down below the horizon, signaling the end of the day, so did it mark the end of my life and the Huron Nation.

EPILOGUE

The next morning some of the Mohawk returned and cut the arrows off even with my back to show respect for me. Otherwise they would have pulled the arrows out to use again. Taking me from the branch, they washed the blood from my face, arms and chest. They dug a shallow grave on a bank, above the swamp, and placed me in it, facing up and toward the swamp. They closed my eyes and on each placed a leaf from the poplar tree so I would see the sky through them. They also placed on my chest the thong of identification made by Fawn, and by my side they put my medicine bag, in case I needed it on my journey to the sky house. They placed nuts, dried meat and water beside me. Then they covered my head with a cloth of cedar bark before covering me with earth. They put stones over me, then more earth. So my life was complete, in accordance with our customs.

About the Author

George McMullen was born in Woodbridge, Ontario, Canada on January 14, 1920. Seeking to avoid ridicule, he kept his psychic gifts secret from the public until he was in his forties.

In 1969 he began working with J. Norman Emerson, Ph.D., an anthropologist/archaeologist at the University of Toronto. For more than 10 years, from 1969 until Dr. Emerson's death in 1978, the two men did research at various Indian sites in southern Ontario, Ohio, and New York state. Dr. Emerson described McMullen's work in numerous papers delivered to professional groups.

McMullen has traveled extensively in Canada and the United States, as well as to Egypt, Israel, France, England, Mexico, Honduras and Ecuador. He traveled in Egypt and Iran with a group headed by Hugh Lynn Cayce of the Edgar Cayce Foundation, researching Cayce's statements regarding those areas. He also worked in Egypt with the Mobius Group, a research organization based in Los Angeles, California. His work there is prominently featured in explorer/author Stephan Schwarz's two books *The Secret Vaults of Time* and *The Alexandria Project*.

McMullen has done extensive criminological work in several states with Ray Worring and Whitney Hibbard, which the two have mentioned in the books they have co-authored, *Psychic Criminology* and *Forensic Hypnosis*.

Articles about George McMullen have appeared in *Fate*, *MacLean Magazine*, *Canadian Heritage Magazine*, and many others.

He continues to work with archaeologists, criminologists and psychic explorers. He and his wife Charlotte currently live in British Columbia.

Red Snake is his first book. He has recently finished a similar work centering on Running Bear, Red Snake's grandson.

What Tom Sawyer Learned From Dying (biography)
by Sidney Saylor Farr

My Life After Dying
Becoming Alive To Universal Love
by George G. Ritchie, Jr., M.D.

Soulmaker
True Stories From the Far Side of the Psyche
by Mike Grosso

The Meta-Human
A Handbook For Personal Transformation
by Paul Solomon

The 365 Reasons Workbook
How To Find A Reason To Be Happy Every Day
by Reba Ann Karp

Healing Feelings, Thoughts & Memories (meditation)
Serene West

Tapping Into The Force (biography)
by Ann Miller and Maxine Asher

Traveling With Power
The Exploration and Development of Perception
by Ken Eagle Feather

Born With A Veil
The Life of a Spiritual Mystic
by Maya Perez with Terry A. Latterman

Contact your local bookseller or write:
Hampton Roads Publishing Co., 891 Norfolk Square,
Norfolk, VA 23502. (800) 766-8009